Readers' Praise for *Hunt for Fred-X*

"Wow! Tom Clancy meets Airplane at Animal Farm!"

". . . a very unique adventure story with an interesting plot, delightful characters, a satisfying ending, and a wonderful Spanish learning experience."

"It's marvelously humorous. If I approved of using the word 'unique,' I'd use it to describe the imagination that produced this tale and the concept it supports."

"A cat-lover's spoof."

"I love this story, and I read it as a novel, not a learning experience."

". . . a fantasy adventure that uses a storytelling technique to teach conversational Spanish in a unique, easy-to-absorb manner."

". . . a simple story for children, an interesting and fantastic spy story for middle or high school students and—for people of all ages—makes Spanish appear accessible, less threatening and demonstrates the reasons we all need to speak it better."

"... a unique way of learning a little Spanish while joining in the adventures of some very lovable animal characters."

"... a wonderful attempt to move across borders and cultures."

"... a fun and educational novel that's approachable at all age levels."

"A fun novel for all ages that teaches you the fundamentals of Spanish."

"Very unique and awesome idea for educational books that can be fun for all ages."

Los Gatos of the CIA: HUNT FOR FRED-X

George Arnold
From an oral account by
Dr. Buford Lewis, Ph.D.

Illustrated by Jason Eckhardt
Translations by August Pieres

NORTEX PRESS  Austin, Texas

Other Books by George Arnold
From Sunbelt Media

Growing Up Simple: An Irreverent Look at Kids in the 1950s
Foreword by Liz Carpenter

BestSeller: Must-Read Author's Guide to Successfully Selling Your Book

This book is a work of fiction, totally the product of the author's imagination. Real characters and locales appear only in a fictitious context. Any resemblance to actual persons, animals or places is purely coincidental.

Typography by Amber Stanfield

FIRST EDITION

Manufactured in the U.S.A.
By Nortex Press
P.O. Drawer 90159 Austin, Texas 78709-0159

1 2 3 4 5 6 7 8 9
ISBN 978-1-57168-861-3
ISBN 1-57168-861-7
Library of Congress Control Number 2005924674

This story is dedicated:

To the notion that we live in a small world, and our brothers and sisters who live across a river or an invisible border, and who may speak a different language, can become our good friends and *compadres simpaticos*, if we all just make the effort to understand one another.

And especially for
Hannah Alicia Norris
Mariel Chun-Shui Clark
and
Julianne Li Ping Clark

* Acknowledgments *

I wish to thank my very smart brother, Bogart-BOGART,* for his unending devotion to proofreading, and my cat friends—Buzzer, Dusty, Luigi and Luisa—and Cincinnati the dancing pig, for allowing me to tell this most amazing story of cleverness in foreign service. I am especially indebted to Dusty Louise for her expert translations and mastery of the Spanish language. Without her help, I would have been *un gran perro payaso*—one big clown of a dog.

Buford Lewis, Ph.D.
Fredericksburg, Texas
2005

*Many have asked me how my brother Bogart-BOGART came by such an odd, repetitive name. He was christened simply "Bogart." Soon, however, we learned of his extraordinary intelligence. Those "smarts" often lead him into deep thought and resulting apparent preoccupation—*él está preocupado*. So to speak. To get his attention, we found ourselves calling, "Bogart. BOGART!" This form of addressing him has become habitual. And remains necessary.

* Contents *

Foreword ix

Cast of Characters xiii

Prologue: The Return of Buzzer Louis, CIA Legend xix

1. *La Locutora* Calls 1

2. Summoning Cincinnati 13

3. Meeting Major *Misterioso* 22

4. *Misilusa* is Missing! 32

5. *Sonora Sam—El Jefe* 48

6. *¡El Cerdo Bailarín Cincinnati No Es Jamón!* 62

7. *La Cucaracha* Has Spoken! 72

8. *El Mayor* on a Mission 83

9. *¡Fiesta!* 96

10. *El Señor Luigi—Un Técnico Muy Excelente* 111

11. *La Chocolatada, Reina de Todos Los Gatos Del Yucatán* 123

12. *¡Libertad, Sí! ¡Aruba, No!* 137

13. *La Gran Sorpresa Final* 147

14. *Gracias a Los Cuatro Gatos Amigos Tejanos* 156

Epilogue: *En La Casa de Las Colinas, Otra Vez* 169
Gracias, Amigos 179
Glossary of Useful Everyday Spanish Words and Phrases 183
About the Authors 199

* Foreword *
It's a Small, Small World

George Arnold has asked me to write an introduction to this most unusual book for one very simple reason. We first met, and have crossed paths occasionally since the time when I had the privilege of serving as president of Rotary International, a post that George knew in some way rivals that of the Secretary General of the United Nations when it comes to traveling the globe and getting to know, up close and personal, some of the most outstanding personalities worldwide. Rotary International is a 100-year-old apolitical, non-sectarian organization in 166 countries, and with more than 1.2 million members dedicated to making the world a better place for every man, woman and child.

George felt that my experience as past president of Rotary International would give me a special—even privileged—worldview that few are ever lucky enough to be able to experience. He knew that, as I visited virtually every corner of the globe, I had come to realize that no matter where we are from, we all have similar types of ambitions. Take away the veneers of suspicion toward one another's motives, differences in dress, culture, and language as barriers to international acceptance, understanding and—ultimately—friendship, and it will be visible to us that all people of good will everywhere have similar dreams and hopes, as well as aspirations for their children, and a desire to live in peace and security.

Indeed, I truly did learn these things and found them to be true.

What George tries to show through his book is that we are all more similar than different. All this based on what he was able to learn in the remote deserts of my country, Mexico. What I personally observed everywhere I traveled was that once we begin to really communicate and work together for similar causes, there is no limit to the good that can be accomplished. In a very unique way, he chose to illustrate this fact by the use of animals—cats, dogs, dancing pigs. Animals who, being naturally curious and lacking the human traits of suspicion and distrust, go about the serious international business of bringing a dangerous rogue to justice in a spirit of trust and cooperation—trust that grows as each learns to speak the other's language.

And in the process, for those who may be interested in being able to communicate on a simple, and trusting, level, he introduces enough useful words and phrases in my native tongue, Spanish, to allow English speakers to travel and converse comfortably, in any Spanish-speaking country. Because being able to communicate is the basic foundation for the beginning of trust and understanding.

You can be sure, there are fun and laughs aplenty in this

unusual spoof. And why not¿ It is, after all, a parody infused with satire, and carried out by animals.

Animals, which we humans can learn much from.

So ... *bienvenidos a este libro. ¡Y disfruten de una buena lectura!*

Frank J. Devlyn
Mexico City
2005

Frank Devlyn is a native of Mexico, a respected optical entrepreneur and an internationally known philanthropist. He is the author of *Frank Talk and Frank Talk II*, both of which tell of his experiences in service to the human family through Rotary International. He lives in Mexico City and travels the world.

* Cast of Characters *

STARRING

Buzzer Louis: Black-and-white tuxedo cat from the Texas Hill Country. Retired former Director of Operations (DO) of the CIA—Cats In Action. World famous for tracking down and doing in desperados and other evildoers. (The "Louis" is pronounced "Lewis." And, yes –it's intentional: you *will* begin to detect a pattern of naming similarities here, as you read on.)

Cincinnati: Dancing pig and former CIA contract operative who is Buzzer's close friend and fellow foe of international criminals and all bad guys.

Dusty Louise: Shy and somewhat petulant, but very pretty, gray tabby cat. Buzzer Louis's younger sister and speaker of the Spanish language.

Luigi and Luisa: Tiny, orange tabby, twin siblings of Buzzer Louis and Dusty Louise. While Luigi is bright and impulsive, even a bit funny, Luisa is thoughtful and deliberate. Both are just babies.

SUPPORTING CAST

Bogart-BOGART: Chocolate Labrador retriever and very smart brother of Buford Lewis, Ph.D. Both Buford and Bogart-

BOGART live on a small ranch in the Texas Hill Country with Buzzer, Dusty, Luigi and Luisa.

Buford Lewis, Ph.D.: Professor *emeritus* and holder of the Rin Tin Tin Chair of Letters at the University of California at Barkley. A white Labrador retriever known as *The Hillbilly Literati.*

Fred-X: Giant and very evil spotted owl, whose guise as a parcel-toting bird of prey provides the perfect cover for his latest penchant—kidnapping Mexican cats, taking them to the Yucatán, and selling them into slavery.

Señora Kay Tal: Diminutive law enforcement officer of the *Federales*—Mexican national police agency.

Mayor Misterioso: Well-intentioned and dim-witted, but high-ranking, officer with the *Federales*.

Sargento Pablo García: Short, stocky *Federales* officer and partner of *Kay Tal.*

CAMEO APPEARANCES BY

Bob the troll: Small ranch hand who manages the business of Buzzer Louis's ranch, and lives in a travel trailer in Buzzer's barn. Bob is given to erratic—even undependable—behavior at times.

Bonzo: Cincinnati's very English butler.

Chocolatada: The most beautiful cat, a calico, in all the *Yucatán*. *Chocolatada* is the first cousin of *Mayor Misterioso.*

Vicente Fox: President of the Republic of Mexico.

La Cucaracha: Wise old *curandera* (medicine woman) of the Primos Indian tribe.

Señora La Locutora: Tall, mysterious emissary from President Fox, sent from Mexico to recruit Buzzer Louis and

Cincinnati the dancing pig to help the *Federales* capture the evil Fred-X.

Señorita Margarita: Very beautiful, but not so honest, young daughter of the chief of the *Primos* Indians.

Misilusa: Sacred cat of the *Primos* Indian tribe. A pawn in Fred-X's latest scheme.

Sonora Sam: Old and grizzled chief of the *Primos* Indians.

Señor Tal Vez: Shady partner in crime with Fred-X in cat-nabbing capers. He sells kidnapped cats into slavery in Aruba.

Taxista Tomás: Fastest taxi driver in all the *Yucatán*.

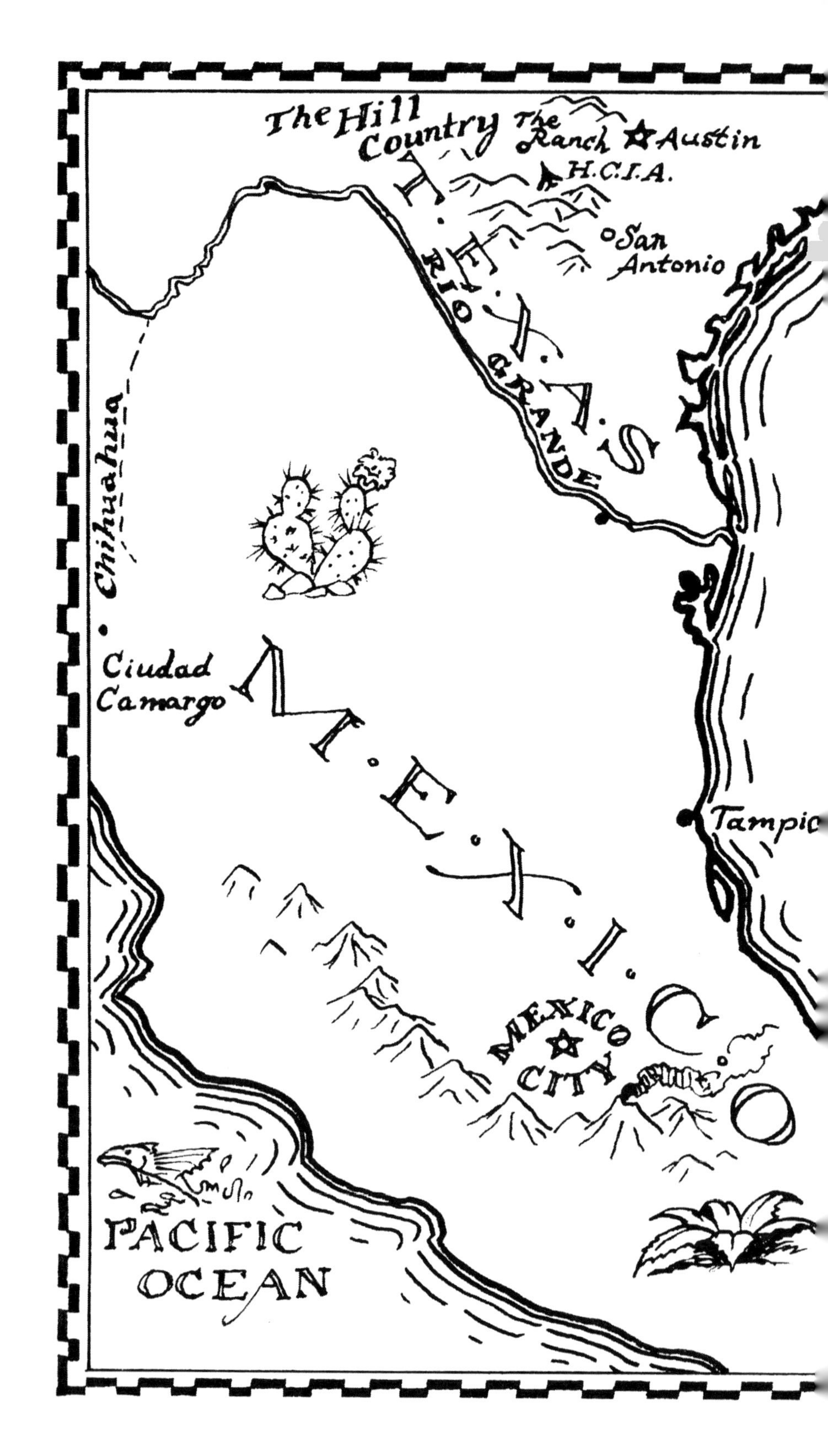

The Hill Country
The Ranch
Austin
H.C.I.A.
San Antonio
TEXAS
RIO GRANDE
Chihuahua
Ciudad Camargo
MEXICO
Tampic
MEXICO CITY
PACIFIC OCEAN

MEXICO & NEARBY TEXAS

THE TRAVELS OF LOS CUATRO GATOS TEJANOS AND CINCINNATI, THE DANCING PIG.

J.C. ECKHARDT, CART.

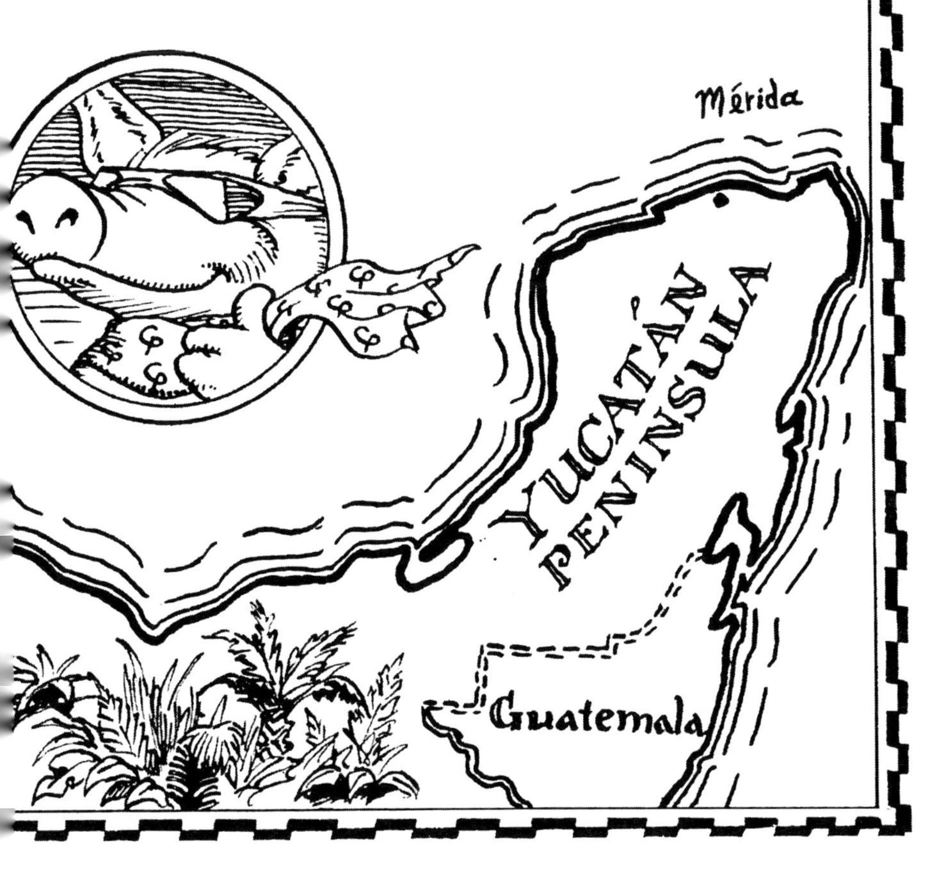

* Prologue *
The Return of Buzzer Louis, CIA Legend

Having observed, while governor of Arkansas, that animals often are more trustworthy than humans, and that cats especially have an innate ability in diplomatic relations that most bipeds seem to lack—former U. S. President Bill Clinton, immediately following his inauguration in 1993, established by executive order a covert branch of the State Department known as the CIA (Cats In Action).

Socks, masquerading as the innocuous Clinton family cat and personal pet of the first daughter Chelsea, headed this small organization, operating quietly and secretly from the White House basement. In truth, Socks led a vigilant and effective international force dedicated to goodwill and understanding by dealing with rogue governments and treacherous operatives throughout the world, bringing them to justice, or very bad ends, whichever came first.

Socks selected, and the Senate's foreign affairs committee secretly confirmed, Buzzer Louis, fearless crime-fighting tuxedo cat from Texas, as the CIA's first Director of Operations (DO/CIA). Buzzer quickly became a quiet legend, bringing down, one after another, bad characters with evil intentions.

In France, Buzzer was known as *le chat*, and earned the French Legion of Merit for rooting out a deadly gang of lemmings in the Bordeaux that sought to corrupt the French language by shamelessly Anglicizing word after formerly pure French word.

In Asia, where he smoked out the rich and elusive, opium-smuggling panda, Ar-Chee, he was hailed as *Delta-One-Yankee-Mao.*

Argentineans revered him as *el gato negro y blanco supremo* after he and his friend, CIA contract operative Cincinnati the dancing pig, set up a national tango and wine tasting *fiesta* to catch and imprison the infamous and slippery *Carlos* the Puma.

In the hushed hallways of Vatican City, Buzzer was whispered to be *sua eccelenza, il gatto magnifico* after he and Cincinnati, posing as fresco restoring painters, nabbed a would-be papal assassin carrying plastic explosives to the pope mobile, the pontiff's little bulletproof Mercedes bubble-car.

Russians and Germans simply called him *Dr. DNA* after he and Cincinnati ferreted out former *Stasi* executioners turned to plying their trade for the Russian Mafiosi.

He had been to Buckingham Palace, where he was made a *Knight of the Realm, Sir Buzzer Louis*. In gratitude for the honor, he had frightened a little mouse under a chair. And, privately, he reported that the entire Windsor family gave him "the creeps."

Yes, Buzzer Louis, master of disguise, known by many identities throughout the world, had clearly become one of a kind, and the best of *the best* of his craft.

Buzzer's fame in the U.S. was late in coming, but his last adventure as DO/CIA, before retiring, earned him the Presidential Citation, and established a domestic reputation that has followed him to his peaceful and secluded retirement in the Texas Hill Country.

Shunning fame and notoriety, Buzzer Louis has taken up an agrarian lifestyle, raising hay to feed the livestock of the area, and breeding registered half-Arabian horses. He has surrounded himself with family—sisters and brothers—and friends from his life before CIA. The semi-sedate life of a gentleman farmer suits him.

Now, however, his last nemesis as DO/CIA, the internationally infamous Fred-X, evil and giant spotted owl whom he brought down and banished with the help of his friend and CIA contract operative Cincinnati the dancing pig, has resumed his wicked ways, stealing Mexican cats and flying them nightly to the *Yucatán*, where he sells them into slavery in *Aruba* with the help of the slippery *Señor Tal Vez,* kittynapping Caribbean slave trader.

The *Federales*, Mexican national police, have appealed to *El Presidente Fox,* the president of Mexico, to invite-entreat-cajole-inveigle, whatever it takes, to get Buzzer to "saddle up" one last time to help them find Fred-X, bring him to justice, and end the spree of 'catnapping' that has plagued Mexico for months on end.

Our story begins with a visit to the little Hill Country ranch by a tall and mysterious emissary from the federal government of Mexico, with a special invitation to Buzzer Louis from *El Presidente,* himself.

¡Vámosnos!

* Chapter 1 *
La Locutora Calls

Luigi Panettone Giaccomazza and his tiny twin sister, Luisa Manicotti Giaccomazza, strained to see out the window of their new ranch house, staring in open-mouthed wonder. They had never seen such a sight.

"It's as long as a fire truck!" Luisa exclaimed.

"Longer than that!" Luigi corrected her. "Look, Luisa, it's got four doors on each side."

The little orange tabby kittens watched as a long, black stretch Lincoln limousine slowly passed by on the road in front of their house. Then, to their everlasting amazement, the big car slowed and turned—right into their winding driveway.

"Buzzer Louis! Dusty Louise! Buford Lewis! Bogart-BOG-ART! Bob! Come over here!" Luigi mewed, roll-call fashion, in his squeaky kitten voice. "The biggest car in the world is coming down our road!"

The biggest car in the world slowly crunched to a stop on the gravel near the house as the four Hill Country cats, Bob—the tiny resident troll, and two extraordinary dogs peered out the window. The driver's door opened. A chauffeur in a blue suit and cap stepped out, walked briskly around the car and opened the last door on the right side of the limo. He leaned into the back seat, and said something the occupants of the ranch house couldn't hear. Nor would most of them have understood his comments if they had been able to hear them.

"Who's he talking to¿" It was Dusty Louise, Buzzer Louis's pretty gray sister, ever anxious to get directly to the bottom of any scene.

"To whom is he speaking¿" Buzzer Louis corrected Dusty's grammar.

"Yeah. Right. Exactly what I said," Dusty responded.

"Give it up, Buzzer," Buford Lewis suggested. "She's never going to speak as eloquently as Dr. Doolittle would like," he scoffed, in reference to the theatrical production they all had attended the night before.

"Look!" Luisa jumped up and was pointing, eyes bulging.

A very tall woman had stepped out of the back seat of the limousine. Stylishly dressed, all in black, she wore a hat with a veil that completely covered her face. As she started across the long front porch toward the red main door, Bogart-BOGART suggested they all hide so she wouldn't know they were staring at her through the window. He had been attempting to be more socially polished, like his older brother, Dr. Buford Lewis.

Four cats, two dogs and a tiny troll scrambled for hiding as the mysterious visitor reached into her purse, took out a card and an envelope, and pushed the doorbell.

Everybody wanted to see what she was doing at the ranch, but nobody wanted to answer the door.

"You get it, please, Bob," Buzzer Louis asked the little troll, their friend who lived in a travel trailer in the big red barn out behind the house.

As Bob opened the door, all six members of the Hill Country peanut gallery crowded behind him, looking over his shoulders.

"Welcome to our little ranch," Bob said, politely.

Buzzer Louis was relieved. He was never quite sure what Bob might say. Sometimes Bob was not as polite as he should be.

"How may we help you¿" Bob went on, assuming his most gracious personality.

The mysterious lady in black lifted the veil from in front of her eyes, slipped on a pair of reading glasses and held a card in front of her—the card she had just taken from her purse.

"Hello," she read, speaking with an accent only Dusty Louise seemed to recognize.

"My name is *la señora*[1] *Locutora,*" she continued reading from the card, "and I am looking for *el señor Buzzer Louis.* I have a personal message for him from the president of the Republic of Mexico."

"Holy *frijoles*!" Luigi Panettone Giaccomazza exclaimed, drawing an instant look of reprimand from Dusty Louise.

La señora Locutora went on reading the card, seeming not to notice little Luigi's inappropriate outburst. "I am to deliver this letter to Mr. Buzzer Louis and await his reply to our president. I do not speak English well."

"That's it!" Bogart-BOGART, being very smart, had already figured things out. "She's from Mexico, and she has a letter from President Fox of Mexico for Buzzer Louis," he said.

---

1. Mrs. Announcer

"Do come in," Bob pulled the big, red door open wide and, surprisingly, continued his mannerly behavior. "Would you like some tea¿ A *taco*¿ Some *menudo* and refried *frijoles*, perhaps¿"

Bob began slipping into his true personality.

Buzzer Louis stepped forward, both to let *la señora Locutora* know his identity and to stop Bob before his next comment created an international incident.

"I am Buzzer Louis," he announced. "Please come in and sit down while I read the letter you've brought to me."

Everyone trooped into the great room except the chauffeur, who remained outside, almost at attention, by the open back door of the big Lincoln.

As they took their seats on two facing leather sofas in front of the tall stone fireplace, *la señora Locutora* read again from the card in her hand. "I am to be sure I give this letter only to Buzzer Louis," she read in her lilting accent. "Would you be so kind as to show me your left front paw, sir¿" she said, addressing Buzzer directly.

The flashback to that cold, rainy night in Hong Kong hit Buzzer like the head-on spray from a fire hose.

The claw.

Stuck—no, imbedded—in that sinister face peering at him through the glass door as the subway raced pell-mell through a pitch-black tunnel.

He remembered now.

Remembered how Cincinnati the dancing pig had cleverly, even deviously, lured the evil panda Ar-Chee from the sumptuous dinner buffet at the luxurious J.W. Marriott Hotel overlooking beautiful and busy Hong Kong Harbor. Lured him by pretending to be a Middle Eastern, *femme fatale* belly dancer with a *thing* for Chinese rogues.

Lured him right down to the basement shopping mall where Buzzer lay in wait.

But Ar-Chee had seen the tuxedo cat and made a mad dash for the subway to Kowloon.

Cincinnati, being the nimble sprinter he was, had outraced the evil panda and reached the open car door first, hopping effortlessly inside. Ar-Chee had made the threshold, too, but just as the doors closed. In a desperate move, Buzzer had leaped and slashed at the opium smuggler's face with his left forepaw, burying his claws deeply into the right side of the screaming panda's sinister visage. As the door closed, only Buzzer's left front paw made it through, leaving him hanging outside the train, suspended by the deep hold he had on Ar-Chee's face. And the subway car's door, closed snugly around his elbow.

It was Cincinnati who saved the night and, most likely, Buzzer's life. The dancing pig's poison-tipped parasol, placed gently, but securely and authoritatively, at Ar-Chee's spine, kept the evil panda pinned against the closed doors. One slight push of the spring-loaded button on the handle and Ar-Chee would have been dog food.

Or worm bait.

Buzzer was left hanging, clinging through that door by his claws, one of which was so deeply embedded, the Hong Kong police surgeon had just snipped it off and left it as a reminder to Ar-Chee that opium smuggling is not a very good idea.

"Buzzer, are you okay?" Dr. Buford Lewis tried to break the glassy-eyed stare that had come over his friend, the tuxedo cat, at the mention of the missing claw.

"Fine. Yes, I'm just fine," Buzzer answered, shaking off the vivid, memory-induced trance as if it had been accidentally spilled all over him.

He held out his paw. The one with the missing claw that he had inadvertently and painfully lost back in Hong Kong in 1998. The claw that remained in Ar-Chee's face—giving Buzzer an almost perfect way of identifying himself. For life.

"Sí," la señora Locutora said, under her breath and seemingly only to herself. *"Usted es señor Buzzer Louis, el famoso gato tejano."*[2] She had seen the claw was missing, and knew for sure, she was with the one and only retired Director of Operations of the CIA—Buzzer Louis, Texas Hill Country tuxedo cat.

"You are to respond to this letter while I wait," she continued reading from her card as she handed Buzzer an envelope with a bright, shiny gold seal on the flap.

"Open it, Buzzy. Tell us what it says!" Dusty Louise was almost frantic.

Buzz lifted the gold seal, opened the envelope and removed what appeared to be a short note. "Uh-oh," he said as he looked at the writing. "This letter is in Spanish. I can't read Spanish and *la señora Locutora* doesn't speak English.

"What are we going to do now¿" he scratched the top of his head with the paw with the missing claw.

"Nobody here speaks Spanish," Buzzer continued, mumbling as if to himself.

"No es verdad. Yo entiendo español muy bien. Hablo español, también."[3] Dusty Louise was speaking, and only *la señora Locutora* smiled in understanding.

---

2. Yes. You are Mr. Buzzer Louis, famous Texan cat.

3. That's not true. I understand Spanish very well. I speak Spanish, too.

"Absolutely astounding." Dr. Buford Lewis was truly amazed.

"I didn't know you could understand Spanish, Dusty," Buzz said with obvious admiration. "Would you read this letter to us, please¿" He handed Dusty the note from the president of Mexico.

Dusty Louise cleared her throat, rolled her tongue, held the note in front of her at arm's length, and began to read:

"Estimado señor Louis,

¡Socorro, señor! El gran búho malvado, Fred-X, ahora vive en méxico. Él rapta a todos los gatos méxicanos y hace un viaje al Yucatán. Allá, otro hombre malo, el señor Tal Vez, hace otro viaje con todos los gatos a Aruba.

Venga aquí a méxico, por favor. Ayude a los federales, gato amigo.

Con mucha sinceridad,
Vicente Fox
el presidente de méxico"

Dusty Louise looked up, smiling proudly at her accomplishment, only to see everyone scowling at her.

"What's wrong¿" she asked. "I said I could read Spanish, and I read it. Didn't I¿"

"You read it very well, I'm sure, Dusty. Only problem is, none of us could understand a word of it, of course. Now, would you be so kind as to tell us, in English, what the president of Mexico said in his letter¿" Buzzer was firm, but nice.

"I'm sorry." Dusty was embarrassed. "Let me read it to you in English." She began:

"Dear Mr. Louis,

Help, sir! The big, evil owl, Fred-X, now lives in Mexico. He steals all the Mexican cats and takes them to the Yucatan. There, another bad man, Mr. Tal Vez, takes all the cats to Aruba.

Come here to Mexico, please. Help the federales, my cat friend.

Very sincerely,
Vicente Fox
President of Mexico"

"Yahoo! Another big adventure." Luigi was excited.

"Can we all go, Buzzy¿" Luisa was thinking that a trip to Mexico would be great fun.

"Hmmm," Buzz pondered. "Dusty will certainly have to go. She's the only one of us who understands Spanish. She can be my interpreter."

"Bogart-BOGART and I can't go, unfortunately." Buford Lewis seemed a little disappointed. "We have classes to teach in California over the satellite, and my students at U.C. Barkley need a good dose of Bogart-BOGART's wise insights. But we'll be your contact in the good ol' U. S. of A.," Buford added. "You never can tell when you might need some help from home, especially with that villainous owl, Fred-X."

"What about us¿" Luigi and Luisa cried in unison. "Don't leave us behind, pleeez!"

"Tell you what." Buzzer was in a good mood. After all, it isn't every day that a Texas cat receives a call for help from a foreign president. "All four of us will go, and I'll invite my friend Cincinnati the dancing pig to fly us there in his new airplane."

"Let's call ourselves '*los cuatro gatos tejanos*,'" Dusty said. "It means 'the four Texan cats.'"

Remembering his manners, Buzzer turned to *la señora Locutora* and said, "*Señora*, you may tell your president that, what was it, Dusty¿ *los cuatro gatos tejanos* will be coming to Mexico to deal with Fred-X."

"*¿Sí¿ ¿Viene a méjico el señor Buzzer Louis¿*"[4] She directed her question to Dusty.

"*Sí, señora. Todos nosotros venimos a méjico—los cuatro gatos tejanos,*"[5] Dusty gestured to her *compadres*.

"*Muy bien,*"[6] said *la señora Locutora,* smiling big for the first time. "Now I must read you one more thing, Mr. Louis." She reverted to English, which she read from her card.

"I thank you, and my president thanks you. *El mayor Misterioso*[7] of the *federales,* the Mexican National Police, will be calling you tomorrow to make arrangements. You will be paid handsomely." She tucked her card back into her purse. "*¡Adios! Y vaya con Dios.*"[8]

With that said, *la señora Locutora* stood up, smiled and shook paws with everyone, and marched out to her limousine. The big, black Lincoln left as it had come less than an hour before, crunching gravel under its heavy weight.

Buzzer Louis looked around the big room, as if thinking to

4. Yes? Mr. Buzzer Louis is coming to Mexico?
5. Yes, ma'am. We're all coming to Mexico. The four Texan cats.
6. Very good.
7. Major Misterioso
8. Goodbye! And go with God.

himself, and said, "We have a lot to do. But first, I have to make a phone call. He headed for his small office and the privacy the telephone call apparently would require.

* * *

Who do you think Buzzer is going to call¿ Will Major *Misterioso* really call tomorrow¿ Will our heroes actually go to Mexico¿ And, if they do, will they capture Fred-X and learn to speak some Spanish, too¿

Aprendamos un poco de español.

(Let's learn a little Spanish.)

By Dusty Louise

In English	*In Spanish*	Say It Like This
COUNTING TO TEN		
one	*uno*	OO-noh
two	*dos*	DOSE
three	*tres*	TRACE
four	*cuatro*	KWAH-troh
five	*cinco*	SEEN-coh
six	*seis*	SAYCE
seven	*siete*	see-EH-tay
eight	*ocho*	OH-cho
nine	*nueve*	new-AY-veh
ten	*diez*	dee-EHS
SOME COMMON COLORS		
red	*rojo*	ROW-ho
blue	*azul*	ah-SOOL
white	*blanco*	BLAHN-coh
green	*verde*	VAIR-day
yellow	*amarillo*	ah-mah-REE-yo
orange	*anaranjado*	ah-nah-rahn-HAH-doh
gold	*oro*	OHR-roe
black	*negro*	NAY-grow

* Chapter 2 *
Summoning Cincinnati

Luigi Panettone Giaccomazza and Luisa Manicotti Giaccomazza kept their little kitten eyes glued to the long, black Lincoln limousine until it turned the corner, and was out of sight headed for town.

Luigi was awestruck over the big car.

"When I grow up, I'm going to be rich and drive a big car just like that one," he bragged to Luisa. "It'll take up three parking spaces every time I go somewhere."

Luisa responded, somewhat sarcastically, "Cats don't drive cars, Luigi." Then, in a rather softer voice, because she could see his feelings were hurt, she added, "But if you're *really* rich, you can own a big car like that and hire someone to drive you everywhere. Wouldn't that be nice?"

Luigi was smiling again, but before he could answer his tiny twin sister, Buzzer Louis asked everyone to try to be a little more quiet for a few minutes so he could make an important long distance telephone call to his old friend and former CIA contract operative, Cincinnati the dancing pig.

"You're calling Cincinnati?" Dusty Louise asked with some redundancy. "Would you please call on the speakerphone so we can all hear?"

Buzzer nodded "yes" as he continued to dial, pushing the speaker button and returning the receiver to its cradle. A few beeps later, all could hear ringing from the speaker.

An audible click was followed by "Pig residence. Bonzo, the butler, speaking." Bonzo's British accent was familiar to Buzz, but took all the others a bit by surprise. As they started to comment among themselves, Buzzer put a paw in front of his mouth to signal them to pipe down so he could hear.

"Bonzo, my man! This is Buzzer Louis, the traveling Texas Hill Country tuxedo cat, calling from the ranch. How are you?" Buzzer had become quite fond of Bonzo on his last trip to Ohio.

"Mr. Louis! How nice to hear from you again. And I am fine, just fine, thank you, sir. Would you care to speak with Master Cincinnati? By the way, sir, this connection sounds a bit hollow, if you know what I mean. And I think you do."

"Sorry, Bonzo," Buzzer replied, apologetically. "I have you on a speakerphone so all my friends and brothers and sisters can hear, too. I have here with me my sister, Dusty Louise; my small brother and sister, the twins, Luigi and Luisa; and our friends, Dr. Buford Lewis and his very smart brother, Bogart-BOGART."

"Hello, everyone," Bonzo responded. "I trust you are all fit and happy today? Hold on one moment and I shall summon Master Cincinnati. Nice talking with all of you."

"Why did he say 'all of you'?" Luisa wanted to know. "Can't he say 'y'all'?"

Dusty Louise smiled. "Bonzo is from England, Luisa. Over there, they don't know how to speak English very well."

Luisa was happy with the answer, as happy as if it had made any sense at all. Dr. Buford Lewis just shook his head and rolled his eyes as if to say, *"Dusty, you are ridiculous."*

Just then the phone line clicked and Cincinnati the dancing pig joined the conversation. "Hello to y'all down there in Texas," he said, much to Luisa's delight, and relief. *At least Cincinnati could speak decent English*, she thought to herself.

"What's up, Buzzer¿" the dancing pig wanted to know.

"Well Cincinnati," Buzzer answered, "our old friend, Fred-X,

is at it again, and we were wondering if you'd like to join us in tracking him down once more, and *really* teaching him some manners this time."

"I thought we'd sent him packing down south three years ago¿" Cincinnati asked, seeming puzzled. "Did he come back already¿"

"No, no, Cincinnati," Buzz chuckled. "He's in Mexico, all right, kidnapping cats. Or—'catnapping' so to speak. He is flying them, this time, to the *Yucatán* where they are being smuggled to Aruba. Vicente Fox, the president of Mexico, sent a messenger with a letter asking for my help. Sort of a plea—from a fox to a cat—to ground an evil owl, if that makes sense.

"So all of us cats are going to Mexico to straighten out Fred-X. We call ourselves *los cuatro gatos tejanos*, the four Texan cats. And, Cincinnati, we're all kind of hoping you would be free and interested in going with us. What do you think¿" Buzzer concluded.

"My stars, Buzz!" the dancing pig answered immediately. "Of course I'll go. Wouldn't miss the chance to teach some better behavior to that crazy hoot owl. Remember what we did to him in Ohio¿" Cincinnati chuckled. "And that flight back to the Texas Hill Country must've scorched him right down to his pinfeathers."

Buzzer remembered, all right.

Almost three years ago, he had gone out to the barn after dinner to work on his hobby—building birdhouses—a kind of *come into my parlor* pastime. So to speak.

Suddenly, sand and sawdust were flying, and the sound of a whirlwind descended on him. A huge shadow blacked out the overhead bulbs he was using to light his workbench. Powerful talons the size of butcher knives had seized him and, before Buzz could grab his hammer and fight back, Fred-X was winging away toward Memphis, one savvy tuxedo cat securely in his grip.

Little did the not-too-bright, but plenty evil, Fred-X know that he was messing with the retired DO/CIA—the internationally revered Buzzer Louis. Now, even—*Sir* Buzzer Louis.

For miles, Buzz had played 'possum,' rousing himself only once to keep Fred-X from crashing headlong into a Delta 757 from Los Angeles that was landing to the north on runway 36R at Dallas/Fort Worth International Airport.

By the time they reached the Arkansas border, Buzz had a plan. He tricked Fred-X into releasing his grip, dropping him into a tall pine tree, and sending the big owl crashing headlong, like a pelican landing on concrete.

But Fred-X had escaped and followed Buzzer, who was posing as a rail-riding hobo, all the way to Ohio. Not smart of the big owl, but at least, persistent.

That's when Cincinnati had joined the hunt. The dancing pig and tuxedo cat lured the spotted owl into a clever trap, hiding Buzzer in an air parcel from Memphis to San Antonio, where Fred-X picked it up for delivery to—guess where? Buzzer's very own new ranch house.

Just as the package-delivering owl approached the house, Buzzer had exploded the box in a shower of sky-lighting fireworks and an ear-splitting cacophony of sound effects, sending Fred-X to his wingtips. Causing him to promise to head south to Mexico, and never return.

Never to steal another cat, either.

But now the second promise was broken. Buzzer knew he had a job to do.

"Excuse me?" Buzzer stared at the speakerphone. "I'm sorry, Cincinnati. I was just remembering our last meeting with Fred-X, and I must've lost my concentration. What was it you just said?"

"I said, 'I remember too, Buzz.' Going with you cats down to Mexico is going to be really fun. How soon do we leave?"

"We'll get a phone call tomorrow with instructions," Buzzer said. "Could you be here in the morning, maybe?"

Cincinnati the dancing pig made a mumbling sound as if he were thinking, and then he said, "I'll crank up *The Flying Pig Machine*, my private jet—as you know—about six o'clock in the morning. I'll be at your airport by about eight thirty your time. Will someone pick me up?"

"I'll ask Bob, the tiny troll, to meet you, my friend," Buzzer said. "We're so glad you'll be going with us. See you in the morning, then. Fly safely."

"Good-bye," Cincinnati said.

Dusty Louise dashed forward and spoke up quickly, and entirely too loudly. "Better try *adiós* or *hasta luego*,[1] Cincinnati," she inserted before he could break the connection.

"Righ-to, er, *adiós*, then. And *hasta lumbago* to y'all!" Cincinnati corrected himself.

"*Hasta mañana, señor cerdo bailarín*," Dusty said quickly. "*¡Vaya con Dios, y vuele con los ángeles, amigo!*"[2]

Dusty was obviously putting on a show now, letting Cincinnati know she could understand Spanish.

"Sure, Dusty, and *hasta* whatever! You teach me Spanish, and I'll teach you to dance like you never thought you possibly could." The dancing pig clicked off quickly before Dusty could regale him again with more language lessons.

So—there would be five going to Mexico in search of Fred-X: Buzzer Louis; Dusty Louise, his interpreter; the orange tabby twins, Luisa and Luigi; and Buzz's friend and former contract operative for the CIA, Cincinnati the dancing pig.

---

1. Good-bye or until then.

2. Until tomorrow, Mister dancing pig. . . . Go with God, and fly with the angels, friend!

"¡Caramba! ¡Magnífico!" Dusty clapped her paws together with glee. *"Los cuatro gatos tejanos y el cerdo bailarín. ¡Qué equipo! ¡Qué compañeros!"*[3] She looked around expectantly—and smiled, knowing full well that nobody had much of a clue what she was saying.

"Yes, well, if you say so, Dusty," Buzzer Louis acknowledged her comments, although he had no real idea what she had said. "But right now we must get ready for our trip," Buzz continued. "Bogart-BOGART, please go to the barn and tell Bob we need him to head for the Hill Country Intergalactic Airport at half past eight o'clock in the morning to pick up Cincinnati, the dancing pig. Thank you, Bogart-BOGART."

The big dog trotted off on his assignment, happy to play a part in the upcoming mission.

"We don't have any luggage yet," Luigi said in a worried voice, tilting his head toward Luisa as he spoke to show he was talking about the two of them. "What can we do, Buzzer?"

"¿Ustedes no tienen nada de equipaje, Luigi y Luisa? Me ponen triste. Tal vez se queden en casa, entonces,"[4] Dusty spoke sarcastically to the little kittens.

"Dusty, I don't know what you just said, but I don't think it was nice," Dr. Buford Lewis, whom everyone thought was fast asleep, lifted his head, opened his eyes and answered Dusty's comment. He suspected what she had said might have been mean.

"But I will take the twins to town in the morning to get

---

3. Wow! Great! . . . The four Texan cats and the dancing pig. What a team! What friends!

4. You don't have any luggage, Luigi and Luisa? How sad. Maybe you will stay home, then.

them some nice backpacks. Backpacks will hold enough. You'll all want to travel light," Buford concluded, dropping his head, closing his eyes and beginning to snore right away.

"I want a red one!" Luisa exclaimed excitedly.

"And I want a yellow one!" Luigi put in his bid.

"Una mochila roja y una mochila amarilla," Dusty said quickly. *"Las dos mochilas para los gatitos gemelos de las colinas."*[5]

She was going to keep this Spanish banter up until someone asked her what she was talking about. But nobody else was ready to learn Spanish yet. They had to get ready for their trip. So they continued to ignore her.

Which was making her furious.

Buzzer looked at no one in particular and muttered under his breath, as if to himself, "We're going to have to start to learn from her. But not right this minute."

He headed for the barn to be sure that Bogart-BOGART found Bob and delivered the important message about picking up Cincinnati in the morning.

* * *

Will Bob the troll remember to pick up Cincinnati at the airport in the morning? Will Luigi and Luisa be able to find red and yellow backpacks at the local department store? Will all five of the adventurers fit into *The Flying Pig Machine*? And what of Buford Lewis and Bogart-BOGART? Will they be able to help from all the way back at the little ranch in the Hill Country?

5. A red bag and a yellow bag. . . . Two bags for the little kitten twins from the hills.

Aprendamos un poco de español

(Let's learn a little Spanish)

By Dusty Louise

In English	*In Spanish*	Say It Like This
DAYS OF THE WEEK		
Sunday	domingo	doh-MEEN-goh
Monday	lunes	LOON-ehs
Tuesday	martes	MAHR-tehs
Wednesday	miércoles	mee-AIR-coh-lehs
Thursday	jueves	HWAY-vehs
Friday	viernes	vee-AIR-nehs
Saturday	sábado	SAH-bah-doh
MONTHS OF THE YEAR		
January	enero	eh-NAIR-oh
February	febrero	fehb-RARE-oh
March	marzo	MARS-oh
April	abril	ah-BREEL
May	mayo	MY-oh
June	junio	HOO-nyo
July	julio	HOO-lyo
August	agosto	ah-GHOST-oh
September	septiembre	sep-tee-EHM-bray
October	octubre	ock-TOO-bray
November	noviembre	noh-vee-EHM-bray
December	diciembre	dee-see-EHM-bray

* Chapter 3 *

Meeting Major *Misterioso*[1]

The tiny orange tabby kittens, Luigi and Luisa, were so excited about their upcoming adventure—the trip to Mexico to find and straighten out that evil, kidnapping, giant spotted owl, Fred-X—that they hardly slept all night.

If the *gatitos gemelos*[2] had only catnapped (in the truest sense of the word), then Bob the tiny troll did not sleep a wink. Bob had earned something of a reputation for being less than dependable, so he was determined not only to pick up Cincinnati the dancing pig as he had been asked to do, but also to be at the Hill Country Intergalactic Airport (HCIA) a half-hour early, at eight o'clock.

It was, in fact, 8:02 A.M. when Bob pulled into the parking lot at HCIA. He smiled to himself as he stepped out of his peculiar orange trollmobile and headed for the terminal.

---

1. Mysterious
2. twin kittens

It was a small, but proud, moment for Bob. He was at the airport, and he was almost a half-hour early!

Good that he was early, too, because just as he crossed the sidewalk to the front door of the HCIA terminal, he heard the unmistakable sound of a sizable airplane landing—tires screeching on asphalt and the high-pitched whine of twin fan-jets, thrusters reversed to help slow and stop the craft. Shading his eyes with one hand and looking into the early morning sun, he saw a beautiful private Sabreliner with the words "*The Flying Pig Machine*" artistically painted below the pilot's side window. It taxied along the tarmac to a parking space not far from the terminal.

Cincinnati the dancing pig had arrived, and Bob the troll was on time to meet him.

"It's going to be a good day," Bob thought to himself.

Meanwhile, back at the ranch, Buzzer Louis and Dr. Buford Lewis had both, unknown to one another, sent Bogart-BOG-ART, Buford's very smart brother, to the barn to see if Bob had left for the airport. Both times the big dog dutifully reported that Bob was nowhere to be found, and that the strange orange trollmobile was gone. While not conclusive evidence that Bob had remembered his mission for the morning, the fact that both he and his car were missing was a good sign.

"It's going to be a good day, Buford Lewis," Buzz said.

"Yes, indeed, a good day, Buzzer," Buford agreed.

"*Sí, un buen día. ¡Hoy es glorioso! ¡La vida es bonita!*"[3] Dusty Louise had resumed her monologue in Spanish, but everyone continued to ignore her.

---

3. Yes, a good day. Today is glorious! Life is beautiful!

Just as Dusty was about to give up and just plain ask why nobody was paying attention to her Spanish, the telephone rang. Glancing at the caller ID, Bogart-BOGART, Dr. Buford Lewis's very smart younger brother, announced that the call was coming from Mexico.

"It must be Major *Misterioso* of the *federales*,"[4] Bogart-BOGART said.

Buzz punched the answer button so everyone in the great room could hear the phone caller. Then he said, "You have reached the ranch. This is Buzzer Louis, traveling Hill Country tuxedo cat, speaking. Good morning, Major *Misterioso*."

"Buenos días, señor gato que trajo su esmoquin. Me llamo mayor Misterioso de los federales. ¿Habla usted español, señor?"[5]

Dusty stuck out her lower lip in a clumsy pout, looked directly at the speakerphone, and said quickly, "Tell him, 'No. Only Dusty Louise speaks Spanish here, and right now she is not inclined to translate.'"

Dusty was upset about her Spanish being ignored all morning.

"Very well, then, *señor* Louis. I shall speak English. Perhaps *la señorita*[6] Dusty Louise will help me if my vocabulary falters. *¿Verdad?*"[7]

The Mexican *federal* major had heard Dusty's petulant comment, and he responded without waiting for an answer to his earlier question.

Buzzer took control of the conversation.

---

4. Mexican national police

5. Good day, Mr. Cat who brought his tuxedo (tuxedo cat). I am Major *Misterioso* of the federales. Do you speak Spanish, sir?

6. Miss

7. Right?

"Major, we are prepared to come to Mexico today to meet with you about hunting down that evil owl, Fred-X. Our good friend, Cincinnati the dancing pig, will bring us to your country in his beautiful airplane, *The Flying Pig Machine.* Where would you like us to meet you, Major¿"

"These arrangements are most convenient, *señor* Buzzer Louis. I am calling from *Chihuahua*[8] because Fred-X was last seen here. Perhaps your friend Cincinnati could fly all of you to *Ciudad Camargo,*[9] where we could meet at the airport later today, maybe at about five o'clock in the afternoon. *¿Está bien¿*"[10] Major *Misterioso* asked.

"Unless it's a problem for Cincinnati, we will see you there, Major. Why don't you give me your cell phone number so we can reach you if plans need to be changed¿" Buzzer Louis suggested.

While Buzzer Louis and Major *Misterioso* were exchanging telephone numbers, and the major was telling Buzz about the tourist cards they would all need to receive once they arrived in Mexico—Luisa and Luigi were involved in a hot discussion.

"But he said he was a dog, or in a dog, Luisa. I'm suspicious of that," Luigi frowned.

"I heard what he said, Luigi, and it worries me, too," Luisa responded. "Some dogs, like Dr. Buford Lewis and Bogart-BOGART, are fine. But those little yapping Taco Bell© dogs can be mean. I don't want anything to do with any Mexican chihuahuas," Luisa crossed her arms and stuck out her chest. She was not going to compromise.

---

8. name of a state in Mexico
9. Camargo City, Mexico
10. Is that all right¿

The *gatitos'*[11] confusion would keep them busily in discussion most of the morning. In fact, they were so wrapped up in trying to figure out if Major *Misterioso* might be a chihuahua that they completely missed the arrival at the ranch of the orange trollmobile. And they almost forgot the promised trip to town for their new red and yellow backpacks.

Bob had retrieved Cincinnati the dancing pig and returned to the little ranch by way of downtown, to give *el cerdo bailarín*[12] a quick tour of their little village.

As they walked across the long front porch of the ranch house, and approached the red front door, Buzzer Louis heard them talking.

"You know what, Bob¿" Cincinnati said.

"What¿" The tiny troll was exhausted from his sleepless night, and was struggling to pay attention.

"What this town needs is a good dance studio. I'm going to call Bonzo and get him started researching the market. I wouldn't mind having a business here. We could open Cincinnati Number 114, right here in the Hill Country."

Cincinnati, who already owned 113 dance school studios in the Midwest, went on talking—as much to himself as to Bob, whose eyes had glazed over.

"No, sir, Bob. I wouldn't mind at all. In fact, a new dance studio here would give me a good reason to come to see all of you—or y'all, as you would say—at the little ranch every so often. The more I think about it, the better I like the idea," Cincinnati said as he glanced at Bob. "Maybe you could run it for me. That is, my tiny troll friend, if you can stay awake."

---

11. kittens

12. the dancing pig

Bob collapsed into a big rocking chair on the front porch, and instantly fell fast asleep, unaware he had just been offered not just a job, but also an entirely new career.

Buzz opened the front door to rescue Cincinnati from Bob's snoring and to welcome him to the little ranch.

"Cincinnati, my *amigo,*[13] please come on in," Buzzer said. "We're just getting ready to go. I've heard from the federales, and they want us to fly to *Ciudad Camargo* to meet them at five o'clock this afternoon. Can you do that?" Buzz asked, almost breathless.

"Be cool, Buzzer," Cincinnati advised. "Let's have a cup of java, look at some maps and get a flight plan ready. Then I can tell you if we can get there by five or not."

"Buenos dias señor cerdo bailarín," Dusty Louise walked into the conversation. *"¿Cómo está usted? Bien, yo espero. ¿Y cómo está su avión? ¿Hay bastante gasolina?"*[14] Dusty Louise was determined somebody was going to pay attention to her Spanish.

Cincinnati responded without missing a beat, "Dusty Louise, I can do the macarena in my sleep. I can mambo on the ceiling. I can even do a fast hat dance, blindfolded. Without so much as stepping on the hat. But I can't understand one word you are saying."

Dusty looked pleased and, yet, somewhat chagrined at the same time. She realized maybe she had gone too far. And so, apparently, did Buzzer Louis as he stepped into the middle of the conversation.

"Dusty, we are all so proud of you for being able to speak

13. friend

14. Good day, Mister dancing pig. . . . How are you? Good, I hope. And how is your airplane? Is there enough fuel?

Spanish. As a matter of fact," Buzzer continued, "our entire expedition to catch Fred-X would be in real trouble except for your bilingual abilities. But you seem to forget that none of us share your talents at the moment.

"You see, Dusty, a translator's job is to make talking easier, not harder. Your job will be to help us understand our friends in Mexico and to help them understand us. It's not to try to confuse. Understand¿" Buzzer concluded, gently, but firmly.

"Lo siento,"[15] Dusty blurted out. "I mean, I'm sorry," she corrected herself. "I'll teach you to speak Spanish, Cincinnati, and maybe you can teach me to fly an airplane. And even to dance."

"Very good, Dusty Louise." Buzzer praised her, and she smiled. "Now please go and tell everyone to be ready to leave for the airport in two hours. Thank you, Dusty."

"Buford Lewis and Bogart-BOGART have taken Luigi and Luisa to town to buy them *mochilas*, er—backpacks," Dusty slipped again. "I'll tell them to get ready as soon as they return."

The little ranch was a beehive of activity. Mostly. Bob the tiny troll was snoring like a miniature chainsaw—or maybe a gasoline powered model airplane—on the front porch, absently swatting horseflies away from his face as he slept.

Buzz had finished packing the night before, so he and Cincinnati were able to concentrate on finding *Ciudad Camargo* on a map of Mexico, and to prepare a flight plan.

When Luigi and Luisa returned from town with Buford Lewis, Bogart-BOGART, and two new backpacks—one yellow and the other red—they busied themselves packing. But both still seemed to be worried about Major *Misterioso*.

15. I'm sorry

"Can a little Taco Bell dog be a policeman¿" Luisa asked for the fourth or fifth time.

"I guess such a little dog could be a policeman, Luisa," Luigi said, "but surely not a *federal*. Maybe a local constable or deputy sheriff, but, no, definitely not a *federal*."

"I just hope we didn't understand right, and that he's not a chihuahua," Luisa sighed. "Those little dogs look like big rats, and I'll bet they smell, too."

"They probably do smell, but I think you mean 'stink.'" Luigi challenged his twin's vocabulary.

"Whatever, Luigi," Luisa sighed again, lifting her eyebrows and looking askance at her brother as if he might be just a tad nutty.

Or at least, a hopeless nitpicker.

"All aboard for the airport." Bob was awake and stomping through the ranch house, rounding up everyone for the short drive in the trollmobile to HCIA.

Dr. Buford Lewis and Bogart-BOGART waved good-bye as the weird orange car pulled out of the long driveway, headed for the airport. Inside the car, Buzzer was attempting to get everyone's attention.

"Okay, listen up!" he shouted, annoying Bob, who did not like loud noises. Especially when he was short on sleep. "Our friend, Cincinnati the dancing pig, has some instructions for all of you," Buzzer said.

All noise stopped. Everyone was paying close attention.

"Thank you, Buzzer," Cincinnati began. "Soon we will be boarding my airplane, *The Flying Pig Machine*, for our trip to *Ciudad Camargo*. Our flying time will be just a little more than two hours. Dusty, our interpreter, will sit in the copilot's seat so she and I can exchange Spanish and flying lessons."

Dusty Louise fairly beamed. She was about to do something very important for the first time in her life.

Cincinnati continued, "Each of the rest of you may sit by a window. But be sure to buckle your seat belts. And do not get up and wander around in *The Flying Pig Machine* unless you ask permission first. We sure don't want anybody getting hurt on the way to *Chihuahua*," he concluded.

"See!" Luigi whispered to Luisa. "He said '*Chihuahua*,' too. That Major *Misterioso* is a Taco Bell dog, for sure!"

"Well, Luigi, he can't bite both of us at the same time," Luisa whispered back. "Let's stick together so we can keep a close eye on him. I don't trust those yappy little dogs. What if he's hairless? Yuck! Nasty looking!"

Luisa turned and looked out the window of the trollmobile nonchalantly, as if she didn't have a care in the world, changing moods as easily as switching on a light.

* * *

But Luigi and Luisa were *really* worried about the Mexican major. Will he actually be a dog? Will he have any hair? Will he try to bite the little kittens?

Will it truly be a good day, after all?

Aprendamos un poco de español

By Dusty Louise

If you are going to be traveling around in a Spanish-speaking country, you will need to know how to say the various forms of transportation. Here are a few for you to learn:

In English	*In Spanish*	Say It Like This
airplane	avión	ah-vee-OHN
train	tren	TREHN
car	auto	ah-OO-toe
ship	barco	BAHR-coh
bus	autobús	ah-oo-toh-BOOS
boat	bote	BOH-tay
truck	camión	cah-mee-OHN
pickup	camioneta	cah-mee-oh-NET-ah
bicycle	bicicleta	bee-see-CLEH-tah

You will also need to know where each of these conveyances might be found.

road/highway	camino	cah-MEE-noh
river	rio	REE-oh
street	calle	CAH-yay
sea	mar	MAHR
stream	arroyo	ah-ROY-yoh
sidewalk	acera	ah-SAIR-rah
path	senda	SEHN-dah
airport	aeropuerto	ah-ehr-oh-PWAIR-toh

Chapter 4
Misilusa[1] is Missing!

"Flying in airplanes is some kind of fun," Luigi Panettone Giaccomazza spoke across the aisle of *The Flying Pig Machine* to his twin sister, Luisa, as the little jet climbed out and away from the Hill Country Intergalactic Airport.

"Yep, Luigi, it sure is. It really is," Luisa responded. "I only wish we weren't going to have to deal with a yapping, snapping little chihuahua dog. Maybe Major *Misterioso* is only half Taco Bell dog. Maybe the other half is Labrador retriever, like Dr. Buford and Bogart-BOGART.

"It could happen," she said resolutely.

Two rows in front of the kittens, Buzzer Louis had lapsed into a deep sleep. He was having something of a surreal dream—a recurring nightmare, actually—about London and Buckingham Palace and the little mouse he had frightened under a chair. Buzz often felt badly about what he did to that mouse, who hadn't done him harm nor wished him bad for-

1. name of a sacred cat

tune. It was just a reflex action, brought on by the pressure of being knighted by a group of royals whom he often professed "gave me the creeps."

In his dream, Buzzer had left the U.S. Embassy with the American ambassador, in a driving rainstorm. Seemed like every time he had been in London, so had the rains. The two arrived at the palace a few minutes early, but managed to get drenched while dashing from the car to the official ambassadorial entrance inside the giant courtyard. The deluge left the ambassador soaked to the skin and in a fine pickle, though Buzzer's tuxedo, which grew on his back, would be quick to dry. Except for the little clip-on bow tie, borrowed from the ambassador for the occasion.

The ambassador's nervousness had rubbed off on Buzzer. Add to the drenching all the confusing and slightly silly pomp and ceremony that accompanied his entrance, and the DO/CIA honoree of the day found himself a little on edge—uncomfortable and, frankly, wary.

He was ushered to a long receiving line of British officials and Windsor family members. It looked to him like a somewhat dangerous gauntlet he would have to run to get to his place of honor before the queen, herself.

As he made his entrance through the long receiving line, politely chit-chatting along the way toward Her Royal Highness, it occurred to him that the whole place smelled musty and dusty, like an incompletely tanned, shriveled-up, old raccoon skin hat that had been left out in the sun in the African desert. He was thinking about that, and trying his best not to sneeze, when he suddenly realized he was at the end of the line—and standing right before Queen Elizabeth II.

Still stifling a mighty urge to sneeze, he remembered to bow deeply from the waist, and then to look up and say, "Your Highness."

The queen cleared her throat, giving forth a most extraordinary sound, a sound not unlike the random and raucous squawking that had pounded his ears the day before as he toured the royal aviary near Hyde Park.

Her Highness began to speak.

"Mr. Buzzer Louis, American citizen and servant to the world, in the name of all that is right and honorable, I welcome you to London and to Buckingham Palace. For international security reasons, I have been advised not to mention that you are the heroic Director of Operations of the clandestine Cats In Action branch of the U.S. State Department. So that shall remain just our little secret," she beamed her finely honed British nasal tones at a crowd of at least five hundred, including press representatives from around the world.

"Great. Just great," Buzzer thought to himself. "She's just blown my cover, and she doesn't even know it."

The queen was droning on … "to this wonderful and reverent moment when it gives me great pleasure and high honor, Mr. Louis, to proclaim you "Sir Buzzer Louis, Knight of the Realm and Protector of the Treasures of Edinburgh, Sydney and Bangkok …"

"Bangkok?" Buzzer thought. "What the devil's she talking about?"

"… and so, with this centuries-old, battle-proven and dreadfully heavy iron sword, I now proclaim you, forevermore, Sir Buzzer Louis, Royal Knight of the Court of Windsor."

Just as the queen reached to tap Buzzer on the shoulder

with the oiled-up old broadsword, the unfortunate happened. A small—and no doubt totally harmless—mouse peeked from beneath the queen's ceremonial robe.

In a flashback to a dangerous encounter in Algiers two years before, Buzz simply reacted without thinking. He stuck out his tongue, crossed his eyes and gave the mouse an old-fashioned Bronx razzberry, complete with an abundance of spittle that made an instant, and very dark, circle on the hem of the queen's gown.

Well, that mouse was frightened, you can be sure. With a mighty "Eeeek!" it dashed from beneath the queen and ran under her royal throne.

If the mouse was frightened, the queen was, shall we say nicely, just plain oblivious. While the entire cadre of press, government officials and courtesans bugged out their eyes and sucked in a collective and highly audible breath—thinking, understandably, that the razzberry had been directed at their queen—Her Royal Highness lightly tapped Buzzer on the shoulder with the sword, handed it off to the Duke of Edinburgh, and then bent and picked up Buzz, cradling him as if he were a royal muff of some kind.

The whole scene was dreadful, of course. And the British press played it for all the sales they could wring out of it. *"Knighted Yank Gives Queen the Razz." "Another Reason Never to Honor a Colonist." "Cat's Caper Stains Queen's Hemline." "Good Road He's Only 15 Inches Tall."*

The ambassador, already a drenched wreck, had to be restrained and hauled off by ambulance to a secure ward "at hospital," as the prime minister recounted.

Despite the hubbub, the queen herself, the Duke of Edinburgh, and the Prince of Wales were completely nonplussed. Ever alert, they had all three missed the entire caper.

The Brits were furious. The mouse swore vengeance. But Buzzer was now Sir Buzzer Louis, Knight of the Realm and Yada-Yada-Yada.

He had to get to a phone and tell the real story to his friend Cincinnati the dancing pig. Cincinnati would roar with laughter, poke some fun at his very English butler, Bonzo, and maybe even create a new dance—*"The Queen's Mouse's Rock."*

"This is your captain speaking." The voice over the intercom startled Buzzer Louis awake. He had been catnapping for more than two hours since *The Flying Pig Machine* had left the Hill Country headed for *Ciudad Camargo*.

Cincinnati continued with his announcement as Buzz blinked his eyes and shook his head, trying desperately to return his mind to the present. "We are ninety-five miles northeast of *Ciudad Camargo* and starting our descent. Please be sure your seat belts are fastened. We'll be landing in about twenty minutes."

Cincinnati the dancing pig eased back on the throttles, raised the speed brakes ever so slightly, and pointed the nose of the sleek jet slightly downward. He was slowing their airspeed and heading directly for *Aeropuerto Ciudad Camargo*.[2]

Suddenly, while Luigi and Luisa continued to quietly discuss what to do about Major *Misterioso* likely being a Taco Bell dog, the twin fan-jets screamed as Cincinnati spooled them up to full throttle, and the little jet lurched violently upward. *The Flying Pig Machine* shot forward, pressing its passengers deep into their seats.

---

2. Camargo City Airport

Then, just as quickly, Cincinnati slowed the plane, re-engaged the speed brakes, and pointed the nose downward again.

"Wow, that was too, too close!" It was the dancing pig speaking into the open intercom, as if talking to himself. "Sorry about that, friends," he said, "but I think we just missed running smack-dab into our old friend, Fred-X. It was a huge bird, anyway, with what looked like something small and black and white in its claws. Gracious sakes, that couldn't be anybody but Fred-X, could it, Buzzer?"

"Had to be Fred-X." Buzzer was a bit more awake now. "At least we have an idea of where to begin looking for him. So he had a black-and-white something in his claws, eh? How high were we when we almost hit him?" Buzzer wanted to know.

"We were just passing through 7,000 feet, Buzz. That's pretty high for a big bird, isn't it?" Cincinnati remarked.

"Well, my friend, Fred-X is not just any big bird, you know. He is something special when it comes to flying high. And not paying any attention whatsoever to airplanes," Buzzer responded.

"*Camargo* tower, this is Sabreliner seven-oh-nine-niner-alpha, five miles northeast on direct, requesting final clearance for runway eight-left." Dusty Louise was on the radio speaking to the airport.

"Sabreliner seven-oh-nine-niner-alpha, you are cleared for approach on runway eight-left. *Bienvenidos a méjico, señorita.*"[3] The radio crackled loud enough for *los cuatro gatos tejanos* to all hear the response from *Aeropuerto Ciudad Camargo.*

"Why are they speaking English¿" Luisa wanted to know.

"All airports in the world use English, Luisa," Dusty responded with a factoid she had just learned from Cincinnati. "I guess there are not enough of us multilingual pilots around these days."

Luigi, paying closer-than-normal attention, just rolled his eyes, wondering if Dusty Louise was letting her first flying lesson go too far to her head.

"Hold tight," the flying dancing pig announced, just as the little jet's tires hit the runway with a screech. It was a smooth landing, following an almost uneventful flight.

"We'll taxi over to the *Pemex*[4] pumps and park so they can top off our tanks," Cincinnati announced. "Someone there will take us to the terminal. Do you know what this Major *Misterioso* looks like, Buzzer¿"

"He's a yapping little hairless, nasty-looking Taco Bell chihuahua!" It was Luigi, voicing his and Luisa's concerns about their soon-to-be host from the *federales*, Mexican national police.

"What¿!! Who told you that¿" Buzzer Louis asked, unbelieving.

"It's true, Buzzer," Luisa piped up. "We heard him. He said

3. Welcome to Mexico, miss.
4. Mexican national oil company

he was a *chihuahua*, or he was in a *chihuahua*. We don't like those nasty little dogs. They can be mean, and we'll have to be too careful."

"No, no, no!" Buzzer was chuckling, but trying not to laugh at the tiny orange pair. "Major *Misterioso* is not a *chihuahua*. He said that he was in Chihuahua—the State of Chihuahua. It's one of the biggest states in Mexico, just like Texas and California are in the United States."

"Okay, Buzzy, but do you really, *really* know for sure he is not a Taco Bell dog¿ I mean, have you actually seen him¿" Luisa remained unconvinced.

"Well, no, Luisa, I haven't seen him," Buzzer answered thoughtfully. "I really have no idea what he looks like, I guess."

"There! You see. That proves it!" Luigi almost exploded in defense of his theory about the Mexican major. "He's a nasty, yapping, little hairless dog with a Snidely Whiplash mustache who wears a black beret, smokes Egyptian cigarettes through a tortoiseshell holder, and will sneak up on you and bite you when you're not looking. We're going to have to be very careful. Very, *very* careful." Luigi's imagination was fueled by watching too many, old Peter Lorre movies on TNT.

"That's *loco*,[5] and you two have gone *chiflado*,"[6] Dusty Louise suddenly joined the conversation. She was looking at *los dos gatitos anaranjados*[7] suspiciously, as if she thought they had lost their marbles. So to speak.

The little jet rolled to a stop. Dusty Louise shut down the engines, and Cincinnati the dancing pig opened the door and re-

5. crazy
6. nutty
7. the two orange kittens

moved his white designer flying scarf and leather helmet with goggles, all at the same time. "You guys stay here for just a New York *minuto, por favor,*[8] and I will arrange to get us to the terminal."

With that, he bolted down the stairs, headfirst, landing lightly on the tarmac on one front hoof and pirouetting gracefully as only an accomplished dancer, or athlete, could do.

"Listen for yapping." Luigi wasn't going to give up his fears about Major *Misterioso* easily.

"Why don't you just wait until we meet the major, Luigi," Buzzer suggested. "Maybe you'll really like him, and maybe he won't be a chihuahua dog at all."

Luigi and Luisa had shouldered their new *mochilas.*[9] Luisa's was *roja,*[10] and Luigi's was *amarilla.*[11]

They were ready for action.

Just then, Cincinnati called out from the bottom of the plane's stairs, "Last one down, turn out the lights. They want us to park right here, and we have a ride to the terminal, *amigos.*[12]

And what a ride it was!

Another big, long, black, eight-door Lincoln limousine, just like the one that had visited them yesterday at their *hacienda pequeña en las colinas de tejas.*[13] Luigi was so excited that he quite forgot about his chihuahua theory and ran to the limousine, shouting, "My car! My car has arrived. Take us to the terminal in style. Er, please¿"

8. minute, please
9. bags
10. red
11. yellow
12. friends
13. little ranch in the Texas Hill Country

The "please" was really an afterthought, but he said it quickly enough that the Mexican chauffeur likely did not detect the momentary lack of manners by the excited little kitten.

"¡Bienvenidos a méjico!"[14] said the chauffeur as he scurried about opening doors for *los cuatro gatos tejanos* and their pilot friend, Cincinnati—*el señor cerdo bailarín.*[15]

The ride to the terminal was short—too short to suit Luigi, who said he thought he might be able to live in a limousine, using it for his house as well as for his transportation. "After all, it has a refrigerator, a TV, a stereo—even a microwave, and it's almost as big as Bob's travel trailer out in the barn," he reasoned.

Luisa proclaimed him *el gatito loco*[16] for thinking such strange thoughts. "What about a bathroom, Luigi¿" she asked, smugly.

"Just step outside." Luigi answered, grinning.

Luisa was not amused.

As the limo pulled to a stop in front of the terminal, the driver jumped out and began opening doors for them. Alighting from the massive limousine, they were met by a short, pudgy man in green fatigues and aviator sunglasses, and a diminutive lady in blue slacks and a red blazer, holding a black beret in her hands.

"Buenas tardes, y bienvenidos a Ciudad Camargo. Me llamo señora Kay Tal. Y aquí está el sargento García. Pablo García. ¿Quiénes hablan español, por favor¿"[17] She let her eyes roam over the entire group.

---

14. Welcome to Mexico!

15. Mister dancing pig

16. the crazy kitten

17. Good afternoon, and welcome to Camargo City. My name is Mrs. Kay *Tal*. And this is Sergeant Garcia. Paul Garcia. Which of you speak Spanish, please?

Dusty stepped forward. *"Me llamo Dusty Louise, y hablo español bien. Yo soy también una miembra de los cuatro gatos tejanos—Buzzer Louis, Luigi y Luisa Giaccomazza, y nuestro amigo, Cincinnati—el cerdo bailarín,"*[18] Dusty completed the introductions.

To their surprise, *el sargento*[19] *Pablo García* spoke up. "I am learning to speak *Inglés, señorita*[20] Dusty Louise, and I would like to try to tell your pig friend and the four Texan cats what is happening. Okay¿"

"Sí, sargento. Proceda usted, por favor."[21] Dusty responded.

The rotund little sergeant took off his sunglasses and began to speak to the group—in English. *"El mayor*—the major—*Misterioso* sends his apologies for not meeting you in person. About three hours ago, he received an emergency call from Sonora Sam, *el jefe de los Indios Primos*[22]—you would call him 'chief' of the Indians. ¿*Verdad,*[23] Dusty¿"

"Verdad," Dusty answered.

"Los Primos live in *las montañas,*[24] the mountains, to the northeast of *Ciudad Camargo*. Their mascot, I believe is your word, is a beautiful cat *que se llama*—who is called—*Misilusa*. Chief *Sonora Sam* has received a warning that someone will try to kidnap *Misilusa* today.

---

18. I am Dusty Louise, and I speak Spanish well. Also, I am one of the four Texan cats—Buzzer Louis, Luigi and Luisa Giaccomazza, and our friend, Cincinnati—the dancing pig.

19. the sergeant

20. English, miss

21. Yes, sergeant. Go ahead, please.

22. the chief of the Primos Indians

23. Right?

24. the mountains

So the major took our helicopter and rushed to the mountains. He asked that we, the *señora Kay Tal* and I, meet you, see to your needs, and then bring you in our *camión*,[25] our big truck, to the mountain village of *los Indios Primos*. I must tell you in all secret—ah, Dusty, what is the word¿"

"Confidence¿" Dusty offered.

"*Sí. Sí.* In all confidence, Major *Misterioso* is a bit, how would you say, 'clumsy.' Yes, that's it. He is clumsy, not only in the feet, but also in the head. *Por ejemplo*—for example, I mean—when he rushed off from here, he ripped off his beret and tossed it into the air, perhaps to see which way the wind comes from, no¿ But then he left it, and called us to tell us to be sure to bring it to him. He is, just between you and me, what you call a 'bumbling fools,'" Sergeant *García* concluded, and looked at *la señora Kay Tal* for reassurance.

She nodded. "He is a complete idiot, but his wife is the daughter of the vice president of the state of *Tampíco*,"[26] *señora Kay Tal* spoke English perfectly. "So the nitwit holds an important job in the *federales*. Do not concern yourselves, however. We will succeed in our mission. My only job is to keep him busy thinking he is doing something worthwhile, and I do my best to keep him out of the way and in the dark. Do you understand¿" she concluded.

"I believe you have made yourself quite clear, and we understand and appreciate your warning. *Gracias, señora y sargento*."[27] Buzzer Louis took charge of the conversation. "Does anyone have any questions before we get started¿"

25. large truck
26. a state in Mexico
27. Thank you, ma'am and sergeant

"How big is his head, and does he have sharp teeth¿ The major, I mean." It was Luigi Panettone Giaccomazza. "Heck, why beat around the bush¿ Does he have any hair at all¿ Or a skinny tail¿"

"Yo no entiendo. ?Perdóneme, Dusty Louise¿"[28] the sergeant spoke.

Dusty Louise laughed. *"A veces, sargento, nosotros no entendemos tampoco.*[29] Luisa and Luigi are afraid *el mayor* is a chihuahua—a Taco Bell dog."

"¡Ay, ya, ya! ¡Hace chistes! ¡Un perrito Chihuahua! ¡Ja, ja, ja! No, mis amigos,[30] I am afraid the major is too, how you say, 'stupid' to even be a chihuahua. He may bark, but he will not bite. And if he does, you have our permission to bite him back, no¿" Sergeant *García* was thoroughly enjoying the little kittens' fears. He chuckled under his breath.

"What does this beautiful Indian cat look like¿" Cincinnati joined the conversation for the first time. He had been thinking the unthinkable.

"Perchance is she small, and black-and-white¿" he asked.

"Sí, sí. How did you know, *señor cerdo bailarín¿"* Kay Tal responded.

"I'm afraid we may have news of Misilusa based on what we saw not a half-hour ago as we were preparing to land here at *Ciudad Camargo*," Cincinnati said, ominously.

"Oh, my gosh. You don't think what we saw could have been . . . ¿ Oh, no. No, no, no!" Buzzer, now wide awake and back in the present, suddenly looked extremely worried.

---

28. I don't understand. Excuse me, Dusty Louise?
29. Sometimes, sergeant, we don't understand, either.
30. Yikes! That's funny! A little chihuahua dog! No, my friends

At that precise moment, Sergeant *Pablo García*'s cell phone rang.

"*¡Pronto! Sargento García aquí,*"[31] he answered, and then he listened for a short time before ending the conversation silently by closing the little folding phone.

"It was *el mayor* calling. Misilusa is missing!"

* * *

Do you think the small black and white object Cincinnati saw in the big bird's claws could have been Misilusa, *la gata sagrada de los Indios Primos¿*[32] What will the major really look like¿ When will *los cuatro gatos tejanos* finally get a scent of Fred-X¿

---

31. Hello! Sergeant Garcia here
32. the sacred cat of the Primos Indians

Aprendamos un poco de español

By Dusty Louise

You have seen that the Spanish name for 'Paul' is Pablo. What about some other common names in Spanish? How would you say them?

In English	In Spanish	Say It Like This
James	*Jaime* or *Diego*	HY-meh, dee-AY-goh
George	*Jorge*	HOR-hay
Robert	*Roberto*	ro-BEAR-toe
Charles	*Carlos*	CAR-lohs
Christopher	*Cristóbal*	kris-TOH-bahl
David	*David*	dah-VEED
Donald	*Donaldo*	doe-NAHL-doe
Edward	*Eduardo*	ed-WAHR-doe
Frank	*Paco* or *Pancho*	PAH-coh, PAHN-cho
Richard	*Enrique*	ehn-REE-kay
Joseph	*José*	ho-SAY
Joe	*Pepe*	PEP-pay
John	*Juan*	HWAHN
Matthew	*Mateo*	mah-TAY-oh
Peter	*Pedro*	PED-roh
Richard	*Ricardo*	ree-CAHR-doh
Thomas	*Tomás*	toh-MAHS
William	*Guillermo*	ghee-YAIR-moh
Ann	*Ana*	AH-nah
Barbara	*Bárbara*	BAHR-bah-rah

Kathleen	*Catalina*	cah-tah-LEEN-ah
Deborah	*Débora*	DAY-bohr-ah
Elaine	*Elena*	ay-LAIN-ah
Hope	*Esperanza*	es-pair-RAHN-sah
Frances	*Francisca*	frahn-SEES-cah
Elizabeth	*Isabel*	ees-ah-BELL
Linda	*Linda*	LEEN-dah
Louise	*Luisa*	loo-EE-sah
Margaret	*Margarita*	mahr-gahr-EET-ah
Martha	*Marta*	MAHR-tah
Mary	*María*	mah-REE-ah
Rose	*Rosa*	ROH-sah
Sarah	*Sara*	SAW-rah
Susan	*Susana*	soo-SAHN-nah
Sophia	*Sofía*	soh-FEE-ah

* Chapter 5 *

Sonora Sam–El Jefe[1]

El sargento Pablo García and *la señora Kay Tal* insisted on arranging for *los cuatro gatos tejanos y el señor cerdo bailarín,* to check into a hotel for a good night's sleep before leaving *Ciudad Camargo* for the mountain village of *los Indios Primos.*

Daylight was waning, anyway, and the mountain road to the Indians' settlement was treacherous according to *sargento García.* He said he would prefer to get an early start *en la mañana*[2] when there would be bright light for the trip.

"We will—how do you say, Dusty¿—kill *los dos pájaros con una piedra.*[3] Get some rest so you will be fresh and relaxed and we will be able to see *el camino peligroso.*[4] *¿Verdad¿*"

"*Los cuatro gatos tejanos* care only about one *pájaro, señor— el búho criminal gigante*[5] Fred–X," Dusty replied. "But our friend

1. The Chief
2. in the morning
3. two birds with one stone
4. the dangerous road. Right?
5. the giant criminal owl

Cincinnati has been awake since very early this morning. So he must be tired. *¿Verdad¿* Cincinnati." Dusty asked.

"Well, I could use a little shut-eye," Cincinnati admitted. "Flying an airplane all day takes some concentration. And that makes me tired," he said.

El sargento García put two fingers to his mouth and whistled loudly, hailing a taxi. "Holiday Inn, *por favor,*"[6] he said to *el taxista.*[7] "*La señora Kay Tal* and I will be along in a few minutes, Buzzer Louis. Please tell the desk clerk to charge your rooms and a good dinner to the account of *el mayor Misterioso de los federales.* We will join you for dinner in the hotel dining room at 7:30 P.M. Will that be satisfactory, sir?" Sergeant García concluded.

"Right. *A las siete y media en el comedor del hotel,*"[8] Dusty answered for Buzzer Louis.

"*¿Listo¿*"[9] asked the taxi driver.

"*Sí. Vámosnos, señor.*"[10] Cincinnati answered, surprising everyone. "I learned a lot from Dusty on the way down here," he said sheepishly, as if to justify his use of Spanish. "She's a very good teacher and I think she may become a good pilot, too."

Dusty beamed as the little green Volkswagen beetle taxi shot forward into traffic, heading the weary travelers toward hot showers, a good meal and warm beds at the Holiday Inn. Crowded into the back seat of the little taxi, Luigi and Luisa found themselves new perches, one on each of Cincinnati's knees, and just high enough to see out the back windows of

---

6. please
7. taxi driver
8. Seven-thirty in the hotel dining room
9. Ready?
10. Yes, let's go, sir.

the noisy taxi. *El cerdo bailarín* hummed them a little tune and bounced them up and down in time to the melody.

Luigi was particularly enjoying the ride. "This is really fun, Cincinnati. I feel like I'm in hog heaven," he said, grinning his little satisfied smile.

"Don't you be talking 'bout hogs and heaven in the same sentence," Cincinnati responded with a smile of his own.

Even though he was tired to the bone, Cincinnati slept restlessly that night. He lay there, thinking about the underground cell of Bordeaux lemmings and their insidious plot to desecrate the French language by substituting English words. Oh, they hadn't been all that hard to find and straighten out since—as lemmings—they made a flock of sheep seem like insurrectionist revolutionaries.

He recalled how the hardest part of the job he and Buzzer had to overcome was figuring out just how many loose-lipped lemmings there actually were. In tracking them across the wine country, Cincinnati and Buzzer had been puzzled, at first, that they left only one set of tracks—tracks that were deep, to be sure, since they all apparently followed one another single file, stepping only where the lemming immediately in front of them had stepped.

In the end, it was Buzzer's idea to dress Cincinnati up in an oversized lemming suit, attach a sturdy rope harness to him and have him actually lead the column of ill-intentioned creatures off a high bluff, thus ending—once and for all—their absurd attack on the sanctity of the French language. Both Buzz and Cincinnati had been awarded the French Legion of Merit. Privately and quietly, of course, so as not to blow their cover.

The whole experience had been tiring for *el señor cerdo*

bailarín. Occasionally his recollections caused him to toss and turn.

Tonight was one of those nights.

Following a hearty breakfast bright and early the next morning, *los cuatro gatos tejanos* and Cincinnati checked out of the Holiday Inn and waited in front of the hotel to be picked up by *el sargento García* and *la señora Kay Tal.*

"He said they had a big truck," Luisa commented, turning her head and straining to see if she could spot it in the morning traffic.

"I'll bet it's not as big as that black limousine we rode in yesterday," Luigi wagered. "If it weren't for having to deal with a hairless, yapping and nasty little Taco Bell dog, this trip would be about perfect," he changed the subject instantly as only Luigi could do. "I'll bet he smells bad, too."

"He either smells badly or he stinks," Luisa shot back, grinning and getting her revenge for Luigi's comment from the previous afternoon, regarding the proper use of adverbs.

"Luigi, I have told you enough times that *el mayor Misterioso* is not a chihuahua," Buzzer said quietly so nobody else except the *gatitos gemelos*[11] could hear. "Don't you believe me¿" Buzzer asked, politely.

"But Buzzy, you said you've never seen the *mayor*. And we know he wears a black beret. And *el sargento García* and *la señora Kay Tal* said he is really stupid. Wouldn't you expect a nasty little yapping Taco Bell dog to be stupid and wear a beret¿ And wouldn't it obviously be black¿" Luigi tried his somewhat questionable logic on Buzzer and Luisa.

11. kitten twins

"I just don't want you to worry about him, Luisa and Luigi," Buzzer continued. "Even if he is a nasty little hairless chihuahua, I'm sure we can deal with him, and we *will* keep him from hurting you two."

"Promise¿" Luigi asked Buzzer Louis.

"Yes, I promise. Cross my *corazón,*"[12] Buzz committed, making an X on his chest with his left front paw as he ventured into the Spanish language for only the second time. "You don't have to be afraid."

Luigi and Luisa smiled like the Cheshire Cat in *Through the Looking Glass,* knowing Buzzer Louis would protect them from *el mayor Misterioso* ... if he should indeed turn out to be a chihuahua.

Cincinnati the dancing pig had bought a Mexican *sombrero*[13] in the hotel's gift shop. Now he dropped it upside down on the sidewalk in front of the Holiday Inn and was humming a catchy little tune while dancing—ever so gracefully—round and round the hat. *Los cuatro gatos tejanos* picked up the spirit of the moment and began to hum with him. They watched as he danced on hoof points that clicked like *castañetas*[14] on the concrete.

An *anciana*[15]—an old lady—walked by and dropped a coin in his hat. Soon *los dos hombres de negocios*[16]—two businessmen—on their way to work tossed in a handful of coins each. A crowd was gathering, and Cincinnati's hat was filling up

12. heart
13. large hat
14. castanets
15. old woman
16. two businessmen

with shiny coins and a few crumpled *peso*[17] notes. His dancing became almost frantic as the coins piled up. He was perspiring profusely.

"*¡Caramba!*"[18] Luigi pointed excitedly. "Look at all that money, Luisa. Cincinnati's going to be rich in a few minutes!"

"Luigi, do you really think somebody who owns more than a hundred dance studios and his own private jet airplane really needs a hatful of coins¿" Luisa was up to her usual trick of poking pins into Luigi's balloons of wild enthusiasm.

"Then he can give it to me!" Luigi shot back, "and I'll buy one of those long black Lincoln limousines and take up three parking spaces wherever I go."

"Whatever," Luisa said, with a hopeless tone in her voice. "Listen. I hear a big truck." She put her paw behind her left ear to better catch the sound.

Sure enough.

The flapping, hollow sound of a big diesel engine and the grinding of gears was getting louder and louder. Then suddenly from around the corner came a huge green canvas-backed truck, belching fat clouds of smelly black smoke from two pipes sticking up behind the cab. As it rounded the corner, grinding and belching, Buzzer Louis could see that the driver was *la señora Kay Tal*. Sergeant *García* was sitting beside her in the front seat.

"That's my ride," Cincinnati spoke to his admiring sidewalk crowd as he stopped dancing, scooped up the money-filled hat and bowed deeply from his trim waist to the ap-

17. Mexican dollar

18. Wow!

plause of the spectators. "Got to go now. *¡Adios, amigos!*"[19] He turned and joined the four Texan cats, luggage in hand, as they stepped to the curb to climb into the big noisy truck.

"That was quite a show," Buzzer said to Cincinnati. "Have you ever done that before¿"

"Pretty often, actually, Buzz. It keeps my dancing sharp and I give the money to P.E.T.P.—that's Pigs for the Ethical Treatment of Porkers. Last year I collected almost three thousand dollars by street dancing," he said as the *camión grande*[20] stopped, hissed, burped one last puff of black smoke and shuddered into silence.

El sargento García hopped down nimbly and strode to the waiting group. "*Buenos días.*" I hope that you have slept well, my friends, because I have spoken this morning to *el mayor*, and *Misilusa* did not return to the village of *los Indios Primos durante la noche*[21]—during the night. We have our work cut out for us.

La señora Kay Tal was dressed in blue jeans and an orange sweatshirt this morning. She busied herself untying ropes and opening up the back of the truck. "You will ride back here, please," she said in perfect English. "It is not very comfortable, but then it isn't comfortable in the front of the truck, either. I have rigged some *hamacas*[22] for you so the ride won't be so bumpy." She pointed into the back of the *camión* where one extra large and four small hammocks were strung sideways under the canvas.

---

19. Good-bye, friends!
20. big truck
21. the Primos Indians during the night
22. hammocks

"How long before we're at the village of the Indians¿" Buzzer Louis asked her.

"The village of *los Indios Primos* is sixty-five kilometers, or about forty-one of your miles from *Ciudad Camargo*. But the road is bad and narrow. It will take us four or five hours to get there," she answered.

"All right!" Luigi's enthusiasm was about to run away with him once more. "Five hours in a big noisy *camión*. Fantastic!"

"Perhaps you will not think it so *fantástico*[23] after an hour or two," Sergeant *Pablo García* said to Luigi. "But we will try our best to make the ride as comfortable as possible for you."

"Also, you may wish to open *las ventanas*—the windows, Dusty¿—and view the *panorama*. Sergeant García looked questioningly to Dusty for help with his English vocabulary.

"Open the windows—the flaps in the canvas—and look out at the scenery," Dusty offered.

"Sí, sí. The scenery. At times the scenery is quite beautiful. Now if you will climb aboard, we will get underway." The sergeant boosted Luigi and Luisa up and put each in one of the small hammocks.

"As we proceed," Sergeant *García* said, "should you need to stop, or just want to stop, please pull down on this rope." He gave a rope hanging down in the middle of the truck bed a short tug and an earsplitting air horn blasted the silence of the otherwise tranquil street scene.

"¡Silencio, locos ruidosos!"[24] It was the doorman at the Holiday Inn who apparently had been awakened by the blast

23. fantastic
24. Quiet, you noisy crazy people!

of the big air horn. Immediately he saw he was yelling at a truck of the *federales* and shouted again, this time contritely, *"Perdóneme, por favor,*[25] *sargento."*

La señora Kay Tal turned the ignition. The starter growled and the big diesel engine chugged to life, covering the street in front of the Holiday Inn once again with a thick cloud of black smoke. Hammocks swung wildly as the truck ripped through its gears and picked up speed, heading out of town to the northeast and the narrow, dangerous mountain road to the village of *los Indios Primos.*

Both Luigi and Luisa thought the erratic swinging of the hammocks great fun. They made a game of leaping from one hammock to another. Buzzer Louis and Cincinnati the dancing pig were soon fast asleep. But the forward, jerky motion of the truck, combined with the swinging to-and-fro of her hammock made Dusty Louise very queasy.

"Look at me, Luigi," she demanded weakly. "Am I turning green, or what¿"

Glancing at Dusty in mid-leap, Luigi Panettone Giaccomazza landed on Luisa's hammock, turned and answered, "No, Dusty Louise, you're still a gray tabby. Not a speck of green on you that I can see. Why don't you close your eyes and pretend you're in a rowboat¿ Maybe that will help you feel better," Luigi seemed momentarily concerned, then spun around and leaped back onto his own hammock, passing a leaping Luisa in mid-air.

Minutes after the big truck got rolling, *la señora Kay Tal* slowed, shifted and made a right-hand turn off the pavement onto a really bumpy road. The ride quickly became so rough

25. Excuse me, please.

that Luigi and Luisa had to stop their game of leap-hammock after Luigi missed his target twice and landed hard on the wooden floor of the truck bed.

"Let's open the *ventanas*," Luigi suggested and—together—he and Luisa managed to roll up the canvas flaps on one side of the covered back of the truck.

What they saw as they peeped out was eye-popping. All around them were mountain peaks covered halfway to the top with pine forests. Little streams and waterfalls seemed to appear from within the mountains themselves, some of them falling hundreds of feet and landing in a cloud of mist.

The baby orange tabbies thought it the most beautiful sight they had ever seen.

Rocking side to side, grinding and groaning upward, the truck and its motion soon had Luigi and Luisa yawning. Within minutes they joined their other three *compadres*[26] in sleep.

Hour after hour they slept soundly as the ten-wheeled, can-

26. friends

vas-covered *camión* slowly droned its way up, up, up into the silent mountains, leaving the hubbub of civilization behind.

At once, they all awoke with a start. Sergeant *García* had pulled the air-horn rope twice as the big truck neared its destination, the village of *los Indios Primos.*

La señora Kay Tal turned the big truck slowly under the spreading branches of an enormous pine tree near the center of the little town and shut off the noisy engine. Everyone hopped out of the truck to see what would happen next.

Luigi leaned over to Luisa and whispered, "Where's that nasty little *mayor*¿ Watch out for him. Just stay behind me," he concluded with some bravado.

Mostly false, of course.

Buzzer Louis suddenly realized there wasn't a person in sight except for one very old man who was walking slowly toward them, leaning heavily on a long stick he was apparently using for a cane. As he approached looking sad and forlorn, he spoke to *el sargento García.*

"Bienvenidos a nuestra aldea," he said softly. *"Me llamo Sonora Sam, el jefe de los Indios Primos. El mayor Misterioso va a regresar en diez minutos, pero la gata sagrada, Misilusa, todavía no está aquí."*[27]

Dusty began her official job quickly and efficiently, having recovered during her nap from the motion sickness that had afflicted her a few hours before. She began, "The old man is Chief *Sonora Sam*, head of the village. He welcomes us and says the major will be back in about ten minutes or so, but that the sacred cat, *Misilusa*, is still missing."

27. Welcome to our village . . . I am *Sonora Sam*, chief of the Primos Indians. Major *Misterioso* will return in ten minutes, but the sacred cat, *Misilusa*, still is not here.

Then she turned to the chief and said, somewhat formally, "*Me llamo Dusty Louise, gata tejana. Y aquí están mis hermanos, Buzzer Louis, el gran gato blanco y negro, y Luigi Panettone Giaccomazza, el gatito anaranjado. También, le presento mi hermana pequeña, Luisa Manicotti Giaccomazza y nuestro amigo, Cincinnati el cerdo bailarín. Tenemos mucho gusto en conocerle, señor jefe.*"[28]

"Good work, Dusty!" Buzzer was most complimentary of her actions and her initiative. "Please tell Chief *Sonora Sam* we are here to find *Misilusa* and return her to their village—and to stop the kidnapping ways of *el búho criminal gigante,* Fred-X."

While Dusty was relaying Buzzer's message to Chief *Sonora Sam*, the ever-vigilant Luisa spotted a wisp of dust in the distance, coming closer and closer. "It must be the major Taco Bell dog. And it looks like he is riding a burro," Luisa said to Luigi and Cincinnati.

"Ah, yes, it is the major," said Sergeant *García*. "Get ready for *una gran sorpresa.*"[29]

* * *

What will the big surprise be? Will the major be a nasty little chihuahua? Will he have *Misilusa* with him? Is she really missing or just playing games with *los Indios Primos*?

---

28. I am Dusty Louise, Texan cat. And here are my brothers, Buzzer Louis, the large black and white cat, and Luigi Panettone Giaccomazza, the little orange kitten. Also, I present to you my little sister, Luisa Manicotti Giaccomazza and our friend, Cincinnati the dancing pig. We are very pleased to meet you, chief.

29. a big surprise

Aprendamos un poco de español

By Dusty Louise

So far in our adventure we have met several animals. Would you like to know how to say the names of some more animals in Spanish? Here they are:

In English	In Spanish	Say It Like This
cat	gato	GAH-toh
kitten	gatito	gah-TEE-toh
dog	perro	PEAR-oh
owl	búho	BOO-oh
bird	pájaro	PAH-hah-roh
donkey	burro	BOO-roh
pig	cerdo	SAIR-doh
parrot	loro	LORE-oh
bear	oso	OH-soh
eagle	águila	AH-ghee-lah
tiger	tigre	TEE-gray
turtle	tortuga	tor-TOO-gah
wolf	lobo	LOH-boh
snake	culebra	coo-LAY-brah
fox	zorro	SOHR-roh
horse	caballo	cah-BYE-yoh
cow	vaca	VAH-cah
sheep	oveja	oh-VAY-hah
goat	cabra	CAH-brah
skunk	zorillo	soh-REE-yoh
armadillo	armadillo	ahr-mah-DEE-yoh
monkey	mono	MOH-noh

* Chapter 6 *

¡El Cerdo Bailarín Cincinnati No Es Jamón![1]

"Los cuatro gatos tejanos y señor cerdo bailarín, may I present to you my superior, Major *Misterioso* of the *federales." La señora Kay Tal* made the formal introduction of the major to *los vecinos norteamericanos*[2] as the major hopped down off the back of a small burro.

"Tengo mucho gusto en conocerle," the major spoke politely and stuck out his arm to begin shaking paws with the *gringos extranjeros. "Bienvenidos a méjico y gracias por la ayuda."*[3]

Luigi Panettone Giaccomazza and Luisa Manicotti Giaccomazza held both their front paws in front of their mouths and closed their eyes squint-tight to try to keep from laughing.

Dusty was giving the kittens a nasty stare, and she was

1. The Dancing Pig Cincinnati is Not Ham!

2. North American neighbors

3. I am very pleased to meet you . . . yankee strangers. Welcome to Mexico and thank you for the help

about ready to give them each a whack and send them back to the truck.

You see, Major *Misterioso* was not a nasty, hairless, snapping, Egyptian cigarette-smoking, mustachioed, black-beret wearing Taco Bell chihuahua at all.

No.

He was a cat!

But not just any cat.

The *mayor* was enormous—the biggest cat Luigi and Luisa had ever seen. He was all black with a pearly-white smile as wide as Cincinnati's shoulders.

"Do not correct the *gatitos por favor, señorita* Dusty. Let them laugh and enjoy the surprise," the giant major cat said softly. "I was told they expected me to be a Taco Bell dog. "*¡Ay, ya, ya! ¡Qué cómico!*[4] I eat Taco Bell dogs for breakfast five days a week." He grinned a big wide grin, and the sun glinting off his teeth almost blinded the tiny orange kittens.

"Maybe he's going to be okay," Luisa whispered to Luigi.

"All cats are okay, Luisa," he replied. "Some are big and some are small. Some are black and some are white. Some are gray and some are orange, like us. Some are calico and some are tuxedo, like Buzzer Louis. Some are spotted and ..."

"All right, Luigi, I get the picture!" Luisa interrupted her little brother's potentially endless cat inventory recitation.

"But all cats are okay!" Luigi quickly got in the last word. Getting in the final comment was Luigi's self-appointed job.

And he was good at it.

Meanwhile *Sonora Sam* was recounting yesterday's disappearance of *Misilusa*, the sacred cat of *los Indios Primos*.

4. How funny!

"A message was left on my doorstep just before noon yesterday—at least that's when I found it. It said there would be trouble in the *aldea*.[5] *Misilusa* might just disappear before our big feast day," the old chief was saying. "I am an old man—*un viejo*[6]—so I do not scare easily. Still I thought perhaps some care should be taken. My daughter, *la señorita Margarita*,[7] volunteered to keep an eye on *Misilusa*," the chief continued.

"Is that when you called Major *Misterioso*¿" Buzzer Louis asked.

"*Sí, sí.* We have heard *mucho*[8] about the missing cats *en todo el campo*,"[9] the chief said. "But we never thought it would happen to us and our *Misilusa*."

"May we speak with *la señorita Margarita*, chief¿" Cincinnati joined in the conversation.

"*Sí, sí.* I will send someone to get her and bring her here for you," the chief responded.

"I can see it's time for me to take charge here," Major *Misterioso* stepped forward, grinning his broad, bright smile. *La señora Kay Tal*'s eyes rolled back in her head. What it was really time for, was for her to get to work keeping the major out of the way.

"Not yet, my *mayor*," *Kay Tal* said to the major. "First I must give you a complete and very, very long and highly detailed report on everything that has happened since you left us in *Ciudad Camargo* yesterday." She winked at Buzzer as if to say, "I will keep him out of your hair for a while."

5. village
6. an old man
7. Miss Margaret
8. much
9. throughout the country

"Great idea, *Kay*! We can sit on the back of the truck and you can fill me in on all the details," the major said. "The big details and the small details. The important details and the unimportant details. The scary details and the funny details . . . "

The major was sounding like Luigi, but *la señora Kay Tal*, unlike Luisa, had no reason to interrupt his palavering. The longer he talked, the longer it would be before he could possibly interfere with the search for Fred-X.

Dusty had gotten her paws on the anonymous note and was translating it.

"Look at this chicken scratching." She showed Buzzer, Luigi, Luisa and Cincinnati. "And the Spanish spelling and grammar are just awful. I'll bet your old nemesis Fred-X wrote this note for sure," Dusty said as she passed the scrap of paper around.

"Oh, yeah, it's the work of Fred-X, no doubt," Cincinnati said as he studied the note. "When we saw him yesterday in the afternoon, I'll bet he'd just stolen *Misilusa* and was heading southeast with her—straight for the *Yucatán*."

"*¿Qué?*[10] What does that mean?" asked Chief *Sonora Sam*.

"It means that by sometime *en la mañana*,[11] that evil spotted owl, Fred-X, will have taken *Misilusa* all the way to the *Yucatán*,"[12] Dusty Louise answered.

"*¡Muy triste!*"[13] *Sonora Sam* hanged his head, and a tear escaped from the corner of his left eye.

Just then, a most beautiful young woman dressed in a red and white gingham dress and soft white leather slippers and

10. What?
11. in the morning
12. a state in Mexico
13. Very sad!

with a rainbow of wild flowers in her long honey-colored hair appeared at the edge of the group, which by now was sitting in the shade of another huge pine tree.

"She is one of those girls," thought Cincinnati, "who can light up a room just by coming into it. I'd really like to teach her to dance." But he didn't say anything at the moment because the young woman's father was making introductions.

"This is my beautiful daughter, *la señorita Margarita Sonora*," the chief said. "She was with *Misilusa* all afternoon yesterday *¿Verdad, hija?*"[14]

"*Sí, padre. Pero no durante la desaparición.*"[15] She turned to the cats and the dancing pig. "I only turned my back for a moment. And then she was gone," the *señorita* said, looking very sad.

Almost.

"She says she was there all afternoon, but not at the moment *Misilusa* went missing," Dusty said, getting into the swing of being a translator.

"Please tell us the whole story," *el sargento García* asked *la señorita Margarita Sonora*.

"My father got this note. You know about the note *¿sí?* After he read it he asked me to keep an eye on *Misilusa* for the rest of the afternoon. So I went to our town hall where *Misilusa* lives. She was there, all right, and looking just fine. She was sleeping away, so I did not wake her."

"What did you do?" Buzzer Louis asked.

"I painted my ¿how do you say *uñas?*"[22] she looked for help with the English word.

"Fingernails," Dusty chimed in.

---

14. Right, daughter?
15. Yes, father. But not during the disappearance.

"Yes, *sí*. I painted my fingernails. I read a magazine. I listened to the short-wave radio. Then about *las dieciseis,*[16] uh four-o'clock, I heard a loud and peculiar noise outside—a noise like a whirlwind kicking up sand and gravel against the side of the town hall. So I got up and went outside to see what it was."

"And did you see anything¿ sergeant *García* asked.

"*Nada.*[17] Nothing. But when I went back inside the rear window was open and *Misilusa* was missing! *Oh, Santa María,*[18] it is all my fault."

La señorita Margarita was trying very, very hard to seem sad.

Trying too hard, as a matter of fact, to suit Luigi. He leaned over to Luisa and whispered, "She's lying. She's not sad at all. She's just pretending to be sad. Something's up, Luisa, and it's not just the sun in the sky."

"You are so right, Luigi," Luisa answered. "She may be beautiful, but she's a terrible actress. Either she wasn't there at all and she's making up this story—or she was there, and she helped Fred-X kidnap *Misilusa*. I'll bet you anything she's lying."

Meanwhile, over at the truck's tailgate, *la señora Kay Tal* was giving her report to Major *Misterioso*. "And then I shifted down into third gear, let out the clutch and pressed on the accelerator, *mayor*," she was droning. "We had gone three blocks from the Holiday Inn by then," she said. "After the red light at *Calle Doce*,[19] I put the truck back into first gear, let out the clutch and pressed on the accelerator. We started moving," she continued.

16. sixteen—4 o'clock P.M. on a 24-hour clock

17. Nothing.

18. Oh, Saint Mary

19. Twelfth Street

"*Bueno. Muy bueno,*[20] *Kay*. Your report is most excellent. Such detail. Important details and unimportant details. Big details and little details. Scary details and funny details. Details, details, details. You are indispensable, *Kay*," the major beamed. "Please continue, *señora Kay*," he said, rubbing his giant front paw-pads together with relish and sounding for all the world like Luigi describing cats.

La señora Kay Tal gave a sideways glance at the group gathered to listen to *la señorita Margarita*. The group was just out of earshot. She smiled to herself and went on, "In the fourth block past the red light at *Calle Doce* there was a hole in the road, so I slowed down and had to shift back into fifth gear . . ."

This report was going to take longer than the actual trip, but *el mayor Misterioso*, not being the shiniest apple on the tree, was intent on listening to every word.

"We have to tell Buzzy," Luigi insisted softly to Luisa. "Maybe he doesn't know she's lying.

"Psst. PSST! Buzzy. Come over here a minute, please," Luigi whispered.

Buzzer Louis walked slowly over to the *gatitos gemelos*[21] and asked, "What is it, Luigi¿"

"She's lying," Luisa spoke up softly so only Buzzer and Luigi could hear. "She isn't sad at all. And if she painted her fingernails yesterday, she must have spent the entire night last night shucking corn, because they don't look to me like they've been painted in a month.

20. Good. Very good.

21. kitten twins

"A woman sees these things," Luisa concluded.

"So you both think she's lying¿" Buzzer asked the tiny orange tabbys.

"*Sí, sí,* as they say in Mexico," Luigi answered quickly.

"Good," Buzz said. "Because Cincinnati, Dusty and I had already decided she's lying like a rug. I think she may even be a part of Fred-X's gang," Buzzer whispered, and then he walked quietly back to the larger group.

La señorita Margarita was still talking.

"I am so sad because today is our biggest feast day of the year," she went on with her obviously made-up story. "It is St. Swithen's Day and *Misilusa* will miss the festival tonight. She was supposed to have been *la reina*—the queen—of tonight's carnival."

"What do you do at the carnival of the feast of St. Swithen¿" Dusty wanted to know.

"First we dig a big pit and then we build a roaring fire in it. And then we toss in a big pig, roast him and eat him," *la señorita Margarita* explained.

"But *Misilusa* did not have time to find us a pig. Our people are so grateful to you, *los cuatro gatos tejanos,* for bringing us one. And a big one, too. Tender and juicy. Mmmmm. *Muchas, muchas gracias,*"[22] she concluded, licking her lips and looking straight at Cincinnati the dancing pig.

"What you talkin' 'bout¿" It was Cincinnati, and he was getting nervous.

Fast.

Sergeant *García* and Buzzer Louis, both startled, began

22. Many, many thanks.

speaking at once, the sergeant in rapid-fire Spanish, and Buzzer in Hill Country tejano.

But it was Dusty Louise who took control, with authority.

"No es posible, señorita fea. ¡Cincinnati—el cerdo que baila y que vuela en el avión, no es jamón!"[23]

Oh, no!

* * *

What will happen now that Dusty has stood up to the chief's beautiful, but lying, daughter? And even called her "ugly?" Will the Indians roast Cincinnati? Or Dusty, maybe? And what about *el Mayor Misterioso*? Will *la señora Kay Tal* be able to keep the amiable but pretty stupid major busy listening to her report until the others have found Fred-X and rescued *Misilusa*?

23. That's not possible, Miss Ugly. Cincinnati—the pig that dances and flies in an airplane, is not ham!

Aprendamos un poco de español

By Dusty Louise

If you are ever in a Spanish-speaking country, get hungry and want to order some food, you will need to know more than just *jamón*. Here are a few food items you can ask for:

bread	pan	PAHN
butter	mantequilla	mahn-tay-KEE-yah
milk	leche	LAY-chee
cheese	queso	KAY-soh
fish	pez	PEHS
salad	ensalada	ehn-sah-LAH-dah
soup	sopa	SOH-pah
beef	la carne de res	lah CAHR-nay day-REHS
chicken	pollo	POH-yoh
potato	patata	pah-TAH-tah
rice	arroz	ah-ROHS
vegetables	verdura	vair-DOO-rah
fruit	frutas	FROO-tahs
water	agua	AH-gwah
candy	bombón	bohm-BOHN
salt	sal	sahl
sugar	azúcar	ah-SOO-cahr
ham	jamón	hah-MOHN
bacon	tocino	toe-SEEN-oh
catnip	nébeda	NAY-beh-dah
eggs	huevos	WAY-vohs

* Chapter 7 *
La Cucaracha[1] Has Spoken!

If Chief *Sonora Sam* had been *muy triste*[2] about the disappearance of *Misilusa*, the sacred cat of *los Indios Primos*—and he certainly had been—then he was now totally devastated by the scene that had just taken place under the big pine tree in the middle of his village.

When Dusty Louise had stepped forward to protect Cincinnati the dancing pig from being roasted in the tribe's firepit during the St. Swithen's Day carnival, she had called the chief's beautiful daughter, *la señorita Margarita, una fea*—an ugly one.

Holy *frijoles!*[3]

La señorita Margarita had gone berserk at Dusty's remark. She began wailing and screaming and bouncing up and down like a jumping bean. Then she tried to catch Dusty, but

1. The Cockroach
2. very sad
3. beans!

couldn't, thanks to some clever footwork by *el cerdo bailarín* with Buzzer Louis on his back, keeping the screaming *muchacha*[4] away from Dusty.

Finally, the chief's *hija linda*[5] had run down the path toward her house, yelling at the top of her voice, "We will roast you, pig! And eat you! And the little gray cat is road-kill!"

"I just don't know what to do," *el jefe Sonora Sam* was lamenting, almost to himself. "I just don't know what to do."

"About what¿" Buzzer Louis asked.

"Señor gato tejano, there are two problems," the chief answered, looking down at his feet. *"Primero,*[6] nobody has ever spoken to my beautiful daughter the way *la señorita* Dusty Louise just did. Dusty has upset *la señorita Margarita*, who is used to always getting her way. I believe Dusty may have even suggested that *mi hija*[7] might have been less than honest in recounting her afternoon with *la gata sagrada*,[8] *Misilusa.*

"Segundo,[9] nobody has ever said 'no' to her before. Not me. Not her mother. Nobody. She plans to roast your friend Cincinnati, and I do not know what to say to prevent it," the chief said.

An almost unbelievingly wide-eyed Luigi leaned over close to his little twin sister Luisa and whispered, "Luisa, do you know how to spell *'la señorita Margarita*¿' Not waiting for an answer to his rhetorical question, Luigi plunged forward, "You

4. girl
5. pretty daughter
6. first
7. my daughter
8. the sacred cat
9. Second

spell it 's-p-o-i-l-e-d b-r-a-t,'" Luigi opined. "That poor girl has never been told 'no' and she's become at least a monster, maybe even an outright criminal, by always getting her way. And what's that big cat major doing, anyway¿" Luigi concluded, changing subjects, again, as only he could do.

In fact, *el mayor Misterioso* was still sitting on the back of the big *camión* listening to the never-ending report of *la señora Kay Tal*, his back to the group under the pine tree.

"And then we turned off the pavement onto the dangerous little road to this village," she was saying, "and I had to push on the brake with my right foot, shove in the clutch with my left foot, steer with my left arm and shift down to a much lower gear with my right hand. I was very, very busy, indeed, *mi mayor,*"[10] she said as she cut her eyes nervously around to the commotion and screaming coming from the direction of the big pine tree.

She was speaking loudly and shifting about nervously, hoping that the major would not hear the noise, and she was worried about what was happening to cause such an uproar.

10. my major

Back under the big tree, Buzzer Louis was speaking to the chief. "Chief, I'm not sure Dusty did actually say that your daughter was not being honest about her afternoon of watching *Misilusa*, but I will say so now. All of us believe she is not telling the truth, and we are concerned that she may even be in cahoots, so to speak, with that evil owl, Fred-X. I'm sorry to have to say these things, but as the agent of *el presidente Fox de méjico*[11] and as the world's foremost expert on the evil ways of Fred-X, I must be honest with you, sir.

"If we are going to get *Misilusa* back and stop the catnapping—perhaps it is better said as 'stop the kidnapping of cats' in Mexico, then we have to begin to be honest—completely honest—with one another. And we have to begin right now," Buzzer said emphatically.

"El señor gato tejano está correcto, jefe,"[12] said Sergeant *García*. *"Hay cierta corrupción en el cuento de su hija. El cuento no es verdad. Lo siento."*

¿Por ejemplo?[13] The chief challenged the sergeant.

"For example, chief, she said she polished her fingernails, yet they were not polished," Buzzer interjected. "And frankly, sir, her acting skills are terrible. We are all absolutely sure she is not at all sorry about the kidnapping of *Misilusa*. In fact, we're concerned that she may have played a big part in it."

"Those are strong accusations, *señor gato tejano*," the chief shot back in anger. *"Mi hija es perfecta."*[14]

---

11. President Fox of Mexico

12. Mr. Texan Cat is quite right, chief . . . There are some mistakes in your daughter's story. Her story is not true. I am sorry.

13. For example?

14. My daughter is perfect.

"No she is not, chief," Cincinnati joined the debate. "And I say that not completely because she wants to turn me into *jamón*[15] tonight, but also because she is obviously lying to us. She knows more about the kidnapping than she's telling, sir," the dancing pig said as tactfully as possible.

"El cerdo está correcto,"[16] *Sargento García* added. "We must not delay. We must get to the bottom of these lies at once if we are going to have any chance of saving *Misilusa*.

"Of course I want to save *Misilusa*, but I do not want to lose my beautiful, perfect daughter at the same time," the chief almost cried.

"Let me ask you something, chief," Dusty Louise suddenly spoke up, sounding almost wise. "How do *los Indios Primos* solve big problems¿ What have you done before when you weren't sure what was right to do¿" she asked.

"Good thinking, Dusty!" Buzzer Louis said. He was impressed. Maybe the responsibility of being their interpreter was helping Dusty to grow up.

"You are thinking right, *gata tejana gris,"*[17] the chief almost looked relieved as he spoke. He tossed this sad monkey off his own back as he said, "I know what we must do. *Consultaremos con la cucaracha."*[18]

Dusty's eyes bugged out, she threw her head back as if recoiling and said, quickly, "Oh, no, he just said we have to have a discussion with a cockroach, Buzzer. I think he's losing it."

---

15. ham
16. The pig is right
17. gray Texan cat
18. We'll talk with the cockroach.

"Usted no entiende,"[19] the chief said, looking directly at Dusty. *"La cucaracha* is our *curandera*. You gringos might call her our medicine 'man' *¿verdad?"* the chief said. "She is very wise. I depend on her when the ¿how do you say? 'the going gets tough,' I believe," he said.

"Is she a bug?" Luigi wanted to know. "A cockroach, I mean?" he added.

"No, of course not. She was given that *nombre cuando era una muchacha pequeña porque ella siempre estaba correteando como una cucaracha,"*[20] the chief answered.

In his excitement, the chief launched into too much Spanish for many of his listeners to follow. But before Dusty could start to translate, Buzzer Louis stepped in impatiently. "We're burning daylight here," Buzzer said, intending to indicate they had better quit talking—in Spanish or English—and do some scurrying of their own, to get on with the meeting with *la cucaracha.*

"Don't say 'burning,' please, Buzzer. Right now, the word 'burning' makes me a tad uncomfortable, if you know what I mean. And I think you do." It was Cincinnati the dancing pig speaking. "As a matter of fact, I would hope we can avoid all references to heating and cooking for a while," he grinned somewhat nervously.

"There is one other problem, *señor* Louis," the chief said quickly. *"La cucaracha* will not allow so many of us into her chambers. Only five may go," he said.

"We don't want to go!" Luisa said, nodding toward Luigi.

---

19. You don't understand

20. name when she was a little girl because she was always scurrying around like a cockroach

"You guys go right ahead without us. A cockroach more than five feet tall is a little scary, anyway," she smiled sheepishly.

"Okay, you two *gatitos*," Buzzer Louis said. "But stay out of mischief and remember we are visitors here in Mexico and this village. Take care to remember your manners."

"When in Rome, do as the Romans," Luigi fired back with a grin. "We'll act like visitors and stay out of trouble, Buzzer. Now stop wasting time. Go see the cockroach doctor."

As Buzzer Louis, Dusty Louise, sergeant *García*, Cincinnati and Chief *Sonora Sam* turned to walk back into the interior of the village, Luigi said to Luisa, "Why do you think these people need a doctor for cockroaches¿ Do the cockroaches here get sick a lot¿"

"I don't get it either, Luigi," Luisa said. "I could understand needing a doctor or a dentist or a veterinarian. Even a doctor for all bugs, maybe. But a cockroach specialist¿ Makes no sense to me."

"I have an idea, though," Luigi was going to change the subject once again. "We don't have to just sit around, you know. We can be, what does Bob the troll call it¿ Proactive¿ That's it. We can be proactive, Luisa. Listen to this."

He leaned over and whispered into Luisa's ear.

"Great idea, Luigi! Let's do it!" Luisa was enthusiastic.

The *gatitos gemelos anaranjados*[21] jumped up and began climbing to the very top of the big pine tree.

At the back of the big truck, meanwhile, *la señora Kay Tal* was droning on and on with her report, to the delight of the dimwitted Major *Misterioso*.

---

21. orange twin kittens

"Then, you see, *mayor,* we didn't know if we should use turn signals or not on such a deserted road. I mean, after all there was nobody to inform that we were about to turn. I wonder, *mi mayor,* if you turn on your blinkers in the woods and there is nobody there to see them, do they really blink¿" she asked, trying not to laugh.

"That's a very interesting question," the major said, scratching his chin. "I suppose we could test the hypothesis, but then if I looked to see if the lights were blinking, somebody would actually be looking. And that would spoil the test. Hmmm," he pondered.

Suddenly his face lit up. "Make a note, *señora*. We must find a blind person to look at the blinkers to tell us if they are flashing. That way, you see, nobody will actually be looking at them. It will work! Sometimes I amaze even myself with these good ideas," he said, smiling and nodding his head in satisfaction.

"You surprise many of us every day, *mayor*. We often wonder how you are able to get dressed and find your way to work," *la señora Kay Tal* said, mocking the major mightily.

The major just swelled with pride.

Back in the village at the small adobe home of *la cucaracha*, medicine "man" of *los Indios Primos*, the important meeting was well underway.

Dusty was uncomfortable because *la cucaracha* was so terribly ugly. She seemed to be very old, was bent at the waist and her hair was stringy and just hanging here and there, randomly. She had only one tooth in the top of her mouth and two teeth on the bottom. They clicked like crickets when she talked.

Cincinnati the dancing pig was uncomfortable as well—because *la cucaracha* had a wild boar's head mounted on a plaque above her *hogar*.[22] It seemed to Cincinnati that the *javalina's*[23] eyes moved to watch him no matter how hard he tried to hide from their gaze.

El jefe Sonora Sam had explained the dilemma to *la cucaracha.* Buzzer Louis and *el sargento García* had added to the explanation.

Dusty Louise and Cincinnati had remained quiet.

"Let me see if I understand this situation." The old lady drooled out of the corners of her mouth when she talked and her voice sounded to Dusty like the screeching of a rusty old hinge.

"What we have here is a lying, overgrown little brat who always gets her way; a really juicy and delicious looking pig who doesn't want to be roasted and eaten; a missing sacred cat, thought to have been stolen by a giant, spotted and very evil owl to be taken to the *Yucatán* and then smuggled to *Aruba*; and a sniveling chief without the spine of a jellyfish. That about sums it up, hey¿" the old lady looked to Buzzer Louis for confirmation.

She spoke amazingly good *norteamericano*[24] English. Dusty knew why after she saw *la cucaracha's* diploma from Harvard University Medical School hanging on the wall. It revealed that her real name was *Paloma Blanca "cucaracha" Servín de Gonzales*.[25]

22. fireplace

23. wild hog

24. North American

25. Paloma Blanca means "white dove." Her maiden name was Gonzales, and she was married to a man named Servin. She is called cucaracha (cockroach).

"You're right on, mama!" Cincinnati spoke up for the first time, preempting any comment from Buzzer Louis.

"Okay, then, *Sam*, my boy," she turned and addressed the chief. "The answer is simple. Here's what you must do as soon as you can muster up some starch in your backbone."

As she gave the answer, she spoke softly—so softly that only *Sonora Sam* and Buzzer, who were sitting right at her feet, could hear. Sergeant *García*, Dusty Louise and Cincinnati the dancing pig could just make out the eerie clicking of her three lonely teeth—now going at rapid-fire pace.

She spoke for more than a minute.

The chief nodded several times to indicate he understood and, as she finished, she said loudly enough for all to hear, *"La cucaracha has spoken!"*

Buzzer jumped up excitedly and gave her a high-five, saying, "Yes! And we all thank you, *mamacita*."[26]

* * *

What do you think *la cucaracha—la señora Paloma Blanca Servín de Gonzales,* said to Buzzer and chief *Sonora Sam*¿ Will *los cuatro gatos tejanos* and their *amigo*, Cincinnati the dancing pig, be able to do as she said¿ Will Cincinnati really get roasted and eaten¿ What are Luigi and Luisa up to—besides the top of the huge pine tree¿ Will Major *Misterioso* never tire of the ridiculous report from *la señora Kay Tal*¿ And what about *Misilusa*¿ Did *la señorita Margarita* actually help Fred-X kidnap her¿

26. little mama

Aprendamos un poco de español

By Dusty Louise

How would you know what to wear if you were to travel to a Spanish-speaking country? Here are the names of some of the clothing you might want to bring with you or buy along the way:

shirt	camisa	cah-MEE-sah
pants	pantalones	pahn-tah-LOH-ness
belt	cinturón	seen-tour-OHN
skirt	falda	FAHL-dah
blouse	blusa	BLOO-sah
dress	vestido	vess-TEE-doh
jacket	chaqueta	chah-KEH-tah
coat	pelaje	pay-LAH-heh
shoes	zapatos	sah-PAH-tohs
boots	botas	BOAT-ahs
socks	calcetines	cahl-say-TEE-nehs
raincoat	impermeable	eem-pair-may-AH-blay
umbrella	paraguas	pahr-AH-gwas
sweater	suéter	SWET-air
scarf	bufanda	boo-FAHN-dah
gloves	guantes	GWAHN-tays
hat	sombrero	soam-BRAIR-oh
cap	gorra	GOH-rah

* Chapter 8 *

El Mayor on a Mission

"It's time to get rolling!"

Buzzer Louis, pumped up by what he had heard from *la cucaracha, la curandera de los Indios Primos*, was ready to put a plan into action—a plan not only to save *la gata sagrada Misilusa*—but also to trap the evil Fred-X, *el búho criminal gigante.*[1]

Buzzer hopped up on a well-used and battered old pine bench in the town square and started giving directions.

"Dusty Louise, will you please go find Luigi and Luisa? They're important right now if the plan is to work.

"Chief *Sam*, please call your village leaders together and tell them of the two hours' delay in the starting time of the St. Swithen's Day *carnaval y fiesta.*[2] But don't tell anyone why. Also *jefe*, please see that *la señorita Margarita* goes to the chambers of *la cucaracha* and stays there. She must be watched at all times.

1. the giant criminal owl
2. carnival and feast day

"Cincinnati, my friend," Buzzer continued, "you have double-duty to play in this plan. But right now would you please create a new hat dance for the carnival—one that you can do with me on one shoulder and Dusty Louise on the other—without any of us losing our concentration¿ I'll explain everything to you, to *los otros tres gatos tejanos*[3] and to the *federales* in just a few minutes.

"And, *sargento Pablo, señor,* please round up everyone who came to the village either in the *camión* or the *helicóptero.*[4] Tell them we will all meet secretly in the back of the big truck at 2 o'clock P.M. That would be *a las catorce horas*[5] *¿verdad¿*—in about half an hour.

Buzzer was getting breathless, both from issuing instructions and from his excitement about the plan they had hatched with *la cucaracha*.

"What about the goofy major, *señor* Buzzer¿ Do you wish *la señora Kay Tal* to continue to keep him out of the way and out of the meeting¿" sergeant *García* asked.

"No, *Pablo*. We need him. He's an important part of the plan," Buzzer answered.

"I know this is all very confusing right now, but please trust me for a few minutes until we meet in the back of the big truck. Then I'll explain everything about the whole plan. *Gracias, señor,*" Buzzer Louis concluded.

Meanwhile Dusty was off looking for Luigi Panettone Giaccomazza and Luisa Manicotti Giaccomazza who, you will remember, had climbed to the top of the big pine tree.

---

3. the other three Texan cats
4. helicopter
5. at 2 P.M.

And sergeant *García* was quietly spreading the word about the secret meeting in the back of the truck at fourteen o'-clock—*a las catorce horas.*

Cincinnati the dancing pig was working out dance steps by drawing with a stick in the soft, sandy dirt under the pine tree.

With everyone else busy for the moment, Buzzer Louis grabbed his small satellite *teléfono*[6] and quickly dialed the little Hill Country ranch to talk to Dr. Buford Lewis and his very smart brother, Bogart-BOGART. Buzzer wanted to be sure the two of them would be available by the speakerphone to participate in the secret meeting. Buzz thought they might have some good thoughts to add to the plan. And he needed them to take care of a special little job to help in the capture of Fred-X.

Amidst all this hustle-bustle, the ever-patient *señora Kay Tal* was droning on in her so-far successful effort to recite a report that would keep Major *Misterioso* busy and out of the way.

"And so you see, *mi mayor,* we had to stop the truck for *quince o veinte minutos*[7] to let the flock of sheep cross the narrow mountain road. I had to decide whether to turn off the engine to save fuel or leave it running in hopes its noise would hasten the sheeps' progress in crossing. What do you think I should have done, *mayor*¿ she asked, not caring a whit what his answer might be. But knowing if she could get him talking, he would burn up lots of time just babbling along.

"Well, *señora Kay,* that is truly a difficult question," the goofy major responded. "On the one hand, you certainly do not want to run out of diesel fuel. *¡Qué problema!*[8] Yet, on the

6. telephone
7. fifteen or twenty minutes
8. What a problem!

other hand, you really want the sheep to hurry up *¿no?* But on the third hand ... no, wait. The third hand must be a foot. It has to be a foot. Yes, it most definitely is a foot. What was the question, again, *Kay?*"

The not-too-bright major had talked himself right into confusion, which was exactly the state in which *la señora Kay Tal* wanted him to reside, for the time being.

At least until the secret meeting began.

Dusty Louise, having found *los gatitos gemelos anaranjados*[9] in the top of the pine tree, returned to the back of the truck, with the twins in tow.

Sergeant *García* had quietly informed everyone who was invited about the secret meeting, and he was standing behind the green *camión*, listening to *la señora Kay Tal*'s never-ending report. And smiling to himself at *Kay Tal*'s cleverness.

Cincinnati, humming and smiling while moonwalking from the big pine tree to the *camión* with Buzzer Louis, announced he had created the new dance Buzzer requested for the St. Swithen's Day *fiesta* and *carnaval*.

The plan was coming together, and now it was time to tell everyone involved exactly what scheme *la cucaracha* had hatched along with *el jefe Sonora Sam* and Buzzer Louis.

"Is everyone here?" Buzzer Louis peeped into the canvas-covered back of the big truck.

"All present and accounted for, sir," Luigi couldn't resist answering. And saluting. He and Luisa had stopped leaping from hammock to hammock, and both were standing at attention. "Dusty Louise, would you please get Buford Lewis and Bogart-

9. the orange kitten twins

BOGART on the satellite phone¿" Buzz asked as he tossed the small *teléfono* to her. "I want them to hear what's happening. Then be ready to translate to the entire group here, if I can't make the plan totally clear in English. Thank you, Dusty," Buzzer said as he sat down and began to gather his thoughts.

Everyone was on the edge of his or her seat, excited to hear what the plan might be. Even the huge black cat major was paying rapt attention, although *la señora Kay Tal* had to ask him to keep his lips together. You see, when he opened his mouth, his bright smile was almost like a flashbulb going off in the semi-darkness of the inside back of the truck.

"Besides," she whispered to *el sargento Pablo*, "when his lips are together he can't say goofy things." She smiled to herself at the cleverness of her ploy to keep the major sidetracked.

"Now then, everyone pay close attention!" Cincinnati the dancing pig assumed his airplane captain's tone of voice to be sure Buzzer Louis had the undivided attention of everyone who would play a part in the plan.

"Thank you, *cerdo bailarín*," Buzzer acknowledged the dancing pig's help in starting the meeting properly. "Buford Lewis, can you hear us¿" Buzzer queried the small satellite phone Dusty was holding.

"Oh, yes, we can hear, Buzz," Buford responded. "Bogart-BOGART is here with me. Please continue, *amigo*."

"The first assignment is for major *Misterioso*, because he is the ranking officer on this expedition," Buzz began, playing up to the big black cat's huge ego. "It is the most important mission, *mayor*, because if it doesn't work the whole plan will fail. Here is what you must do, *señor*. Walk slowly to the house of *la cucaracha*. Sit down there with *la señorita Margarita* and have a long, quiet conversation. Three times during the discussion, mention that you sure hope that big *búho*, Fred-X, doesn't look in the top of the tall pine tree in the center of the *aldea*[10] during the St. Swithen's Day celebration. Pretend to be very worried that he might come back later tonight and find something in the top of that tree. *¿Comprende, mayor?*[11]

"What will be up in the pine tree?" the major wanted to know.

"Oh, that is top secret, *señor*," Buzzer replied. "Not even *el presidente Fox de Méjico*[12] knows the answer to that. Only *la cucaracha* knows.

"And she will never tell."

"Okay, so I am just to make a long visit with *la señorita* and during that conversation say three times that I hope *el búho criminal gigante* doesn't come back during the *fiesta* and look at the top of the pine tree? *¿Verdad?*"

The major, surprisingly, seemed to understand his assignment perfectly. As he started off toward *la casa de la cucaracha*,[13] Buzzer Louis wished him well, knowing—of course—that even if the major forgot everything, *la cucaracha* would be there to be sure the plan's seeds were planted.

Properly.

"Buena suerte señor, y vaya con Dios."[14] Buzzer said to him. "When you have accomplished your mission, return here to find *la señora Kay Tal*," Buzzer concluded.

---

10. village
11. Do you understand, major?
12. President Fox of Mexico
13. the cockroach's house
14. Good luck sir, and go with God (or Godspeed).

"Bueno,"[15] said the major as he began walking to the medicine woman's house—the home of *la cucaracha* and the temporary holding cell for the suspect *la señorita Margarita*.

"Now," Buzzer said to the group, "since the major is gone we can discuss more openly all the parts of the plan. Here are the assignments:

"First, *jefe Sonora Sam*, we will need you to find two small hollow gourds—about the size of Luigi and Luisa. And a tube of Krazy Glue. *¿Recuerda, señor?"*[16] Buzzer reminded him of the plan he had heard from *la curandera.*

"Sí, sí, señor gato. I will go to get them right away," the chief said, almost excited as he headed off, leaning heavily on his long wooden staff and walking slowly into the forest.

"Second, Buford Lewis and Bogart-BOGART, your assignment is to take down the portrait of me hanging above the fireplace in the great room. Scan it into your computer and e-mail it to the notebook of *la señora Kay Tal*. Her e-mail address is quetal@federales.mex.gov. Did you understand that assignment?" Buzz spoke directly into his small satellite phone.

"Easy enough, Buzz," Buford responded, "but may we stay on the line to hear the rest of the plan?"

"Yes, of course you may," Buzzer answered. "Even Bogart-BOGART will find the plan of *la cucaracha* very clever. Very clever, indeed," Buzz said.

He continued speaking to the group in the back of the big truck.

"Third, here is the assignment for you, *sargento García.*

15. Good.

16. Remember, sir?

Please contact *la oficina de los federales en la Ciudad Camargo*[17] and have them send to us two tiny, but powerful, radio transmitters. We will need two different frequencies, sergeant, both of which may be received by *la radio del helicóptero.*[18] And we will need them before dark tonight. Can you do that, *señor¿*" Buzzer smiled, knowing it was an easy task.

"*Sí, sí, señor* Louis," the sergeant answered as he scrambled from the back of the big *camión's* tailgate and headed for the truck's cab and its powerful radiotelephone to contact his office in the city.

"Fourth," Buzzer continued, "an assignment for *la señora Kay Tal*. "Before the assignment, though, we should all like to say '*muchas gracias*' to you for keeping *el mayor* busy today. *Buen trabajo, señora.*"[19] Buzzer began clapping in appreciation and Dusty Louise, Cincinnati, Luigi and Luisa all joined in.

"*Ahora, señora,*[20] you will need to find a large pair of scissors, four dark buttons and some black thread. Can you find those items, please, and return here by the time the chief gets back with the gourds¿" Buzzer asked.

"*Sin duda, señor gato blanco y negro,*"[21] *la señora Kay Tal* responded. And she started off for the village.

"Now for the assignments for Dusty Louise, Cincinnati and me," Buzzer Louis continued.

"What about us¿" Luigi interrupted. "Don't we have an assignment, too¿ After all, we spent several hours up in the top

---

17. the federales office in Camargo City
18. the helicopter's radio
19. Good work, ma'am.
20. Now, madam
21. Without a doubt, Mr. white and black cat

of the pine tree, keeping lookout for Fred-X, Buzzy." Luigi was almost pleading.

"Don't worry, Luigi and Luisa," Buzzer said, grinning a smile almost as big as that of the goofy major. "Your assignments will require the greatest sacrifice of all," Buzzer concluded.

"But first, Cincinnati has created an exciting new dance for *la fiesta de esta noche,*"[22] Buzz continued. He was starting to pick up some useful Spanish phrases and use them, much to Dusty's delight. "At precisely the right moment during tonight's celebration, Cincinnati will perform his new dance and Dusty will be on one of his shoulders. I will be on the other. Our job is to create a commotion among *todos los Indios Primos*[23] so that everybody is looking at us and nobody is looking at the top of the pine tree. *¿Comprende¿*"[24] Buzz asked.

"That still leaves us out, Buzzy Lou," Luisa said, quizzically. "What are we supposed to do, Luigi and me, I mean," she asked. "What's the big sacrifice we're going to make¿"

"Okay, you two," Buzzer said affectionately, "we need to borrow all your hair!"

"What¿!!"

The two *gatitos gemelos* shouted in unison.

"You want to make us look like nasty, yapping, hairless little Taco Bell dogs¿" Luisa was shocked.

"I said your assignments would require a big sacrifice," Buzzer answered sympathetically. "But you are baby kittens. Your hair will grow right back. And I promise to punish anyone who tries to make fun of you until it does. Will you let us

22. the fair (or feast day) tonight
23. all the Primos Indians
24. Understand?

borrow your hair, please¿ *La señora Kay Tal* will snip it off. And it won't hurt a bit," Buzzer promised.

Luigi stood up tall on his back legs and saluted. "I will do it for the good of t*odos los gatos de méjico!*"[25] he announced proudly.

"Okay. I will too," Luisa said, almost sadly. It was clear to all she was not looking forward to being hairless, even for a week or two. "But you will owe us big time," she reminded Buzzer.

"Well, that's the plan. Does everyone understand it¿" Buzzer asked.

"That's not exactly a plan, *mi amigo,*" Cincinnati spoke up. "A series of assignments, maybe, but not a plan," he looked a little perplexed.

"I know! I know!" It was Bogart-BOGART, the very smart brother of Buford Lewis, Ph.D.

Buzz could imagine that Bogart-BOGART was madly waving a front paw in the air, as if begging permission to speak.

"Would you like to tell everyone¿" Buzz asked Bogart-BOGART, smiling and knowing that the big Labrador retriever had everything figured out.

"Sí, sí," Bogart-BOGART said with a chuckle. "This is, I think, the plan," Bogart-BOGART began. *"El mayor* will let *la señorita Margarita* know there will be something in the top of the big pine tree during the *fiesta*. If everyone is correct about *la señorita Margarita*'s truthfulness, she will guess that Luigi and Luisa will be in the top of the tree since she's seen them there earlier today. So she will call Fred-X and tell him to hurry back to get two cute *gatitos norteamericanos pequeños*[26] while nobody's looking."

"Except¿" Buzzer Louis asked.

---

25. all Mexican cats!

26. little North American kittens

"Except instead of Luigi and Luisa, what will be in the tree will be two gourds with Luigi's and Luisa's hair glued to them. And inside them will be two tiny radio transmitters so y'all can track Fred-X to his hideout in the *Yucatán* and capture him.

"That's about it, right¿ Luigi and Luisa are going to be kidnapped by Fred-X, except they'll really only be substitute hairy little gourds," Bogart-BOGART completed his theory.

"Good. Very good, Bogart-BOGART," Buzzer responded. "Give yourself an extra Milk-Bone© tonight."

"That takes care of everything except our assignment here at the little ranch," Buford said. "Why are we sending your portrait to *la señora Kay Tal*¿ I don't quite see how that fits."

"You are both pretty smart," Buzzer answered. "The picture in *Kay*'s computer will be used later, after we get to the *Yucatán*. It's for what we *gatos hispánicos*[27] call *la sorpresa cómica final*[28]—the final funny surprise—for our old buddy, the wicked Fred-X. But I mustn't give the secret away just yet," Buzzer continued. "Please wait until tomorrow and we'll call you again so you can be in on it. Maybe Bogart-BOGART can figure it out in the meantime."

"You got it, Buzzer," Buford said.

"Now we must go, Buford and Bogart-BOGART. *Hay mucho que hacer antes de la fiesta*,"[29] Buzzer said.

"If you say so, Buzz," Buford responded. "*Adiós y buena suerte, mis amigos*."[30] Buford Lewis clicked off the line and Dusty Louise turned off the little satellite telephone.

27. Hispanic cats
28. the final funny surprise
29. There's a lot to do before the festival
30. Goodbye and good luck, my friends.

Buzzer spoke to the remaining members of the group.

"Now we have to really get busy. Everyone take care of your assignments, and we will meet back here *a las diecisiete horas*.[31] That's five o'clock to you gringos," Buzzer said, laughing.

* * *

Will the major be able to remember to do his part¿ Will the beautiful daughter of *Sonora Sam* fall for the trick and call Fred-X¿ Will Fred-X try to sneak back in the dark to kidnap two hairy gourds, aka Luisa and Luigi¿ What will *la sorpresa cómica final* be¿

Aprendamos un poco de español

By Dusty Louise

Suppose you are in a Spanish-speaking country and you need to go to the doctor. How would you tell him or her what was hurting? Here are some parts of the body in Spanish to help you:

ankles	*tobillos*	toe-BEE-yohs
arms	*brazos*	BRAH-sohs
cheeks	*cachetes*	cah-CHEH-tehs
chin	*barbilla*	bahr-BEE-yah
face	*cara*	CAR-rah
fingers	*dedos*	DAY-dohs
hair	*cabello*	cah-BEY-yoh
hands	*manos*	MAH-nohs
head	*cabeza*	cah-BAY-sah
hips	*caderas*	cah-DARE-ahs
lips	*labios*	LAH-byohs
mouth	*boca*	BOH-cah
neck	*cuello*	KWEH-yoh
shoulders	*hombros*	OHM-brohs
toes	*dedos de pies*	DEH-dohs deh pee-EHS
tongue	*lengua*	LANE-gwah
wrists	*muñecas*	moon-YECK-ahs
stomach	*estomago*	ess-TOHM-ah-goh

* Chapter 9 *

¡Fiesta![1]

While all the *federales* and Luisa and Luigi were carrying out their various afternoon assignments, Buzzer Louis and Cincinnati the dancing pig were sitting on the battered old pine bench in the center of the village, resting up for the long night they expected was right in front of them.

Dusty Louise, having delivered the kittens to the back of the big *camión* and into the hands of *la señora Kay Tal* with her big pair of scissors, wandered up to join them. Dusty couldn't bring herself to watch the twins turn into hairless little creatures.

"You know what this all reminds me of, Buzz¿" Cincinnati had a faraway look in his eyes.

"What, Cincinnati¿" Buzz responded.

"Maybe 'Who¿' would be a better question," Cincinnati said.

"Okay, my twinkle-toed friend, 'Who¿' then," Buzz answered.

"Carlos."

1. Festival!

"You mean the *puma¿*[2] *Carlos the puma¿*"[3] Buzzer's eyelids shot up and he suddenly seemed tense. His eyes darted left, then right as if he'd developed some sort of on-the-spot tic.

"Yep. That's him. *Carlos the puma*. And Argentina. Dance contests. Wine tastings. Tricks and traps, pratfalls and long drops," Cincinnati rattled off seemingly unrelated phrases, all the while watching Buzzer's expression.

Studiously.

At least they all seemed unrelated to Dusty Louise, who stared at the dancing pig, a puzzled expression on her face.

"My gosh, you're right, Cincinnati," Buzzer said, continuing to look about nervously. "I think I'll go check on the twins," he said as he hopped off the bench and started for the back of the truck, moving a little faster than Dusty had seen him move in a long, long time.

"Well, Dusty, I guess he's still not ready to talk about it," Cincinnati said, as if Dusty would have a clue what he was talking about.

"I don't have any idea what you two were talking about," Dusty fessed up.

"About Argentina four years ago, and the final capture of that international menace, *Carlos the puma*," Cincinnati responded, still thinking Dusty would understand everything with that bit of additional information.

"Means nothing to me, Cincinnati," Dusty confessed.

"Oh. Then Buzzer never told you¿"

"Told me what¿" Dusty was feeling completely confused.

---

2. cougar

3.Charles the Puma

"About the night in *Buenos Aires*[4] when he almost was killed."

"No. Almost killed¿" Dusty said.

"Yes. It was a really close call. He's never going to get over it until he's willing to talk about it, though. I thought maybe enough time had passed that we could talk it through. But I guess today's not the day." Cincinnati stared off to the horizon.

"Would you tell me about it¿" Dusty looked worried.

"Will you promise never to speak about it with Buzzer unless I'm there¿" Cincinnati said. "I'd be worried about him unless I was there to catch him if he falls."

"Why would he fall¿" Dusty wanted to know.

"I don't mean literally fall, Dusty. But what happened that night obviously shook Buzzer to the core."

"What happened¿" Dusty asked, adding, "I promise not to ever bring up the subject with Buzzy."

"Okay, if you promise, then."

"*Carlos* had just brought down the fifty-third Italian government since World War II by cleverly poisoning more than a dozen members of the Socialists' party. Oh, all the deaths were ruled 'natural causes,' but Buzzer and I—and worldwide law enforcement—saw clearly the paw prints of *Carlos* all over the death certificates. He had made complete fools of the *carabiniere*—the Italian national police.

"They weren't the first to be fooled by *Carlos*, for sure. Not at all. You could throw in Scotland Yard, Interpol, the FBI, even the KGB. *Carlos* was simply the best—or maybe the worst is a better way to put it—international saboteur ever."

---

4. Good Air, literally. A big city in Argentina

"What happened¿" Dusty was always anxious to get straight to the story at hand.

"Buzzer and I tracked him from *Fiumicino*[5] in Rome to Buenos Aires. For years, Interpol had insisted *Carlos the puma* operated out of a base in Argentina. We saw him on a customs video entering Argentina posing as a Chinese shoe salesman."

"How did you catch him¿"

"Like every high-living bad guy, *Carlos* had his Achilles heels. In his case he was smitten with great wine, and dancing with beautiful women. So Buzzer and I dreamed up a national wine tasting and tango contest. Entries were invited from throughout the Argentine—all of South America, actually.

"We knew he would enter.

"Sure enough, on a night not much different from this one, there he was. Half of couple number fifty-seven in the tango contest.

"His partner was a stunning young Brazilian girl—from *Ipanima*.[6]

"Poetic, no¿"

"I guess so, Cincinnati. But how did Buzz nearly die¿" Dusty pressed for the end of the story.

"Well, Buzzer got himself appointed the head judge of the tango contest. It was held in a big ballroom on the twenty-third floor of the Sheraton Hotel. His job was to ferret out *Carlos* and chase him off the balcony outside the ballroom. I was waiting below with the fire department and the police and a big net. We would catch *Carlos* and wrap him up.

5. International airport in Rome. Another Italian word that means "little river."

6. Name of a beach near Rio de Janeiro, Brazil. A Portuguese word.

"Once and for all."

Dusty interrupted yet again. "What went wrong¿"

"Nothing really went wrong, Dusty. Buzzer, true to his calling, waited patiently for *Carlos* and the girl from *Ipanima* to begin their tango. Then, when they approached the French doors leading to the balcony, Buzzer sprung the trap. He rushed at *Carlos*, and *Carlos*—recognizing the DO/CIA—made a beeline for the balcony.

"Buzzer was right on his tail.

"Then the unexpected happened. The girl from *Ipanima* flung a wine glass in Buzzer's path. He hopped, to avoid the broken glass and, as he slid sideways, he lost his balance and went right on over the balcony rail a few seconds behind *Carlos*.

"It was a long way to the ground.

"And there was only one net ready," Cincinnati continued.

"Couldn't you catch both of them¿" Dusty was concerned.

"Not really, Dusty. *Carlos* fell first. Buzzer was only about halfway down when the net snapped around *Carlos* and his career of crime was over. Buzzer could see below that there was no net to catch him, so he spread out his arms and legs to try to slow his fall. I saw what he was doing and grabbed two flashlights from *la policía*.[7]

"Like a signalman, I guided him into the big fountain in front of the Sheraton where he hit with a mighty splash. A perfect cannonball, as I've often kidded him.

"But it wasn't funny that night. Buzzer was knocked out cold when he hit the water. Problem was he almost drowned. Oh, he had a few bruises, but the water's what almost got

7. the police

him. I pulled him from the fountain and gave him mouth-to-mouth resuscitation.

"We didn't think he was going to make it, but just before we were about to give up, he spit out a mouthful and started breathing again.

"And, do you know what his first words were¿"

Cincinnati didn't wait for Dusty to guess. "They were, 'Did we get *Carlos*¿' I was almost amazed, but I had learned over the years never to underestimate *mi amigo,*[8] Buzzer Louis. He still thinks I saved his life.

"But he won't talk about it."

"What happened to *Carlos*¿" Dusty wanted an end to the story.

"He was tried, found guilty of many crimes and is now serving a life sentence in a Brazilian prison on the upper Amazon River. And good riddance, too," Cincinnati added.

"Wow! Buzz really *is* a hero!" Dusty seemed surprised.

"Indeed he is. On six continents, Dusty. A legend, in fact. Never forget what a special brother you have."

"We better get back to our plans." Dusty had heard the end of the story—a happy ending—and was now ready to get on with the business at hand.

"Righto, Dusty. Let's go find Buzzer. And remember, not a word!"

The entire owl-catching cast had gathered behind the big truck. Members were drifting off to take up their positions assigned in the plan.

As the sun dropped to the top of the mountains and day-

8. my friend

light began to wane, rainbow-colored paper lanterns were strung on ropes surrounding the center of the square of the *aldea* of *los Indios Primos.*

Each lantern held a candle inside that flickered crazily in the mountain twilight.

The fire pit intended for roasting a pig for the *fiesta* had been carefully refilled with dirt so that Cincinnati was a bit more relaxed, seeing in his mind's eye the new hat dance he had created as a diversion for the evening's trap for Fred-X.

To save Cincinnati from the fire pit, *la cucaracha* had declared "Cheese and Tofu Day," and for twenty-four hours *los Indios Primos* would be allowed to eat no *jamón.*[9] *La curandera*[10] had said, with a wink and a smile, that she had looked in the mirror and seen a vision telling everyone to eat no pigs.

Buzzer Louis took out his little satellite telephone and dialed up Buford Lewis, Ph.D. and his very smart brother Bogart-BOGART back at *la hacienda pequeña*[11] in Texas.

He was filling them in on the afternoon's actions.

"The chief found some gourds exactly the size of Luigi and Luisa, and sergeant *García*'s assistants in *Ciudad Camargo* delivered the two little radio transmitters along with a full tank of fuel for *el helicóptero.*[12] We put the radio signalers in the gourds and *la señora Kay Tal* snipped off and glued Luigi's and Luisa's hair to the outside of them," Buzzer told them.

"Dusty Louise took the hairy gourds to the top of the big pine tree," Buzz continued. "In the twilight they look just like

9. ham
10. the medicine woman
11. the little ranch
12. the helicopter

los dos gatitos,[13] but the real Luigi and Luisa are playing leap-hammock in the back of the big *camión*. Bless their hearts, they're hiding so nobody will see them *sin sus pelos*.[14]

"And the best news, Buford and Bogart-BOGART, is that *el mayor* says he heard *la señorita Margarita* pick up her phone and call Fred-X the minute he left her in *la casa de la cucaracha*.[15] Looks pretty clear to me that she is, in fact, in cahoots with Fred-X, and we think he's headed this way. With a little luck, this plan of *la cucaracha's* just may work," Buzzer spoke into his little *teléfono de satélite.*[16]

"Buena suerte, mi amigo."[17] It was Bogart-BOGART speaking; he was beginning to pick up and use some Spanish phrases, too. "We've scanned in your portrait and e-mailed the file to *la*

13. the two kittens
14. without their hair (hairless)
15. the cockroach's house
16. satellite telephone
17. Good luck, my friend.

señora Kay Tal's notebook computer. Now we'll keep our paws crossed and be waiting to hear from you.

"Good luck and good-bye, Buzzer."

As Buzzer put away his little phone, he surveyed the scene before him. Everything was ready. The trap for Fred-X would be sprung soon. Buzz knew he had to shake the morose feelings that the mention of *Carlos the puma* had placed on him, like a wet blanket. One day he would sit and talk about it with Cincinnati, but tonight he had to be alert to take down Fred-X.

El jefe Sonora Sam and his young and beautiful, though wicked, daughter were already seated on a platform above the square. A third chair of honor beside them was reserved for *la curandera.* Cincinnati and Sergeant *García* were boosting her up to the platform.

On the bandstand directly across from the tribe's royal family, the Fabulous Thunderbirds were setting up their amplifiers and testing their sound system. They had flown into *Ciudad Camargo* earlier in the afternoon from San Antonio and ridden up to the village with the *federales* who brought the helicopter fuel and radio transmitters.

The Fabulous Thunderbirds were one of Cincinnati's favorite *tejana-mejicana*[18] bands. They would provide the music for tonight's *fiesta* and—in the morning—ride back to town *en el camión de los federales.*[19]

Dusty wandered up to stand next to Buzz. "Did you get some of that *queso de cabras¿*"[20] Dusty asked Buzz. "I really like

18. Tex-Mex
19. in the federales' truck
20. goat cheese

it," she said, "especially now that it's helped save Cincinnati from becoming a huge platter of *jamón*."

"I did get some, Dusty, and I like it, too," Buzzer said as the Fabulous Thunderbirds—still tuning—launched into the first few bars of one of their *canciones tejanas*.[21] "But that tofu tastes like last week's beans. Ugh!"

"Let's get with Cincinnati so we're ready to do our dance when the major and *Kay* give us the signal that *el búho*[22] has arrived." Dusty still had a bit of hall monitor in her outlook.

Meanwhile, back at the big truck, seemingly unaware of the naked-kitten leap-hammock game going on behind him, *el mayor Misterioso* listened intently to the continuation of what Dusty was now calling *"el informe más largo del mundo"*[23] from *la señora Kay Tal*.

"So when we reached the top of *el paso de los cráneos,"*[24] she droned on, "we could see ahead of us near the bottom of the pass *la famosa curva de los muertos—un sitio muy peligroso*[25] *¿verdad? mayor,"* she asked.

"Sí, sí, Kay. ¡Muy peligroso, de verdad!" the major answered. Then he added, *"¿Pero, porqué se llama 'la curva de los muertos?'"*[27] as if he'd just arrived from another galaxy.

"It is called 'dead men's curve,' *mayor*, because *Pancho Villa*[28] once hid *muchos caballos*[29] stolen from the U.S. Army there,"

21. Texan songs
22. the owl
23. the biggest report in the world
24. skull pass
25. the famous dead men's curve—a very dangerous place
27. But why is it called 'dead men's curve?'
28. Mexican revolutionary folk hero
29. many horses

she answered, knowing it didn't much matter what kind of an answer she provided. The major, she knew, would accept any ridiculous, made-up answer as totally logical and rational.

Being a complete idiot must make life simple, she thought to herself as Luisa missed the hammock she was jumping for and smacked headlong into the major's backside.

He didn't seem to notice.

Back behind the bandstand, Cincinnati, Buzzer and Dusty were practicing *el nuevo baile de los sombreros*[30] quietly in the shadows. "I think we have it down now," Cincinnati said. "You guys balance very well, one on each shoulder. Let's get dressed for the dance," he suggested. "We sure want to be ready when the signal comes."

Cincinnati the dancing pig pulled over his head a silver lamé *camisa del matrimonio mejicano*.[31] Buzzer slipped into a black *toreador*[32] suit with a red sash. And Dusty Louise put on *un vestido blanco con muchas campanas rojas*[33] hanging from its little red belt.

They were ready to perform the spectacular new dance. The signal would come from the major and *Kay Tal*, who had discontinued listening to and reciting their report, respectively, and had trained powerful binoculars through the pine tree to the southeast where Fred-X would likely come from.

"What is the signal, again¿" Dusty Louise asked.

Buzz answered. "*La señora Kay* and *el mayor* will flash the *camión's* high beams twice on the bandstand. That will tell the

30. the new hat dance

31. Mexican wedding shirt

32. bullfighter

33. a white dress with many red bells

Fabulous Thunderbirds to break into our song, and we will leap to the center of *el cuadrado*[34] into two roving spotlights and keep everybody's eyes glued to us until Fred-X has picked up the gourds and headed back toward the *Yucatán*.

"Then we'll all jump in the helicopter and follow him at a safe distance so he won't know we're there," Buzzer explained the logistics to Dusty and Cincinnati one last time.

At the very instant he finished his explanation, the headlights of the big truck flashed twice. The Fabulous Thunderbirds began playing the song Cincinnati had picked out—their old hit, "*Wrap it up, I'll take it.*"

"A fitting song for stealing kittens, no¿" Cincinnati mused.

"We're on!" Buzzer shouted over the amplified sounds of the band. Dusty hopped up on Cincinnati's right shoulder, and Buzzer hopped on his left. Cincinnati leaped into the center of the *cuadrado*, tossed down his big *sombrero*[35] and began to dance like a Tasmanian devil.

Both Buzzer and Dusty were keeping the top of the big pine tree in sight. Although they looked like an acrobatic dance troupe, only Cincinnati was actually dancing. Dusty pirouetted in her little white dress with the red bells on one of his shoulders and Buzz, pretending to be facing *el toro,*[36] turned on the other shoulder, so the two of them were always looking at the tall tree.

"It's working!" Buzzer shouted into the dancing pig's left ear. "Every eye in the place is on us!"

"Yes, and there's Fred-X!" Dusty shouted into Cincinnati's

34. the town square
35. hat
36. the bull

other ear. "He's falling for it! He's grabbed the two hairy gourds and is spinning away into the night!"

As the song ended and the dancing trio came to a stop, *todos los Indios Primos comienzan a aplaudir,*[37] shouting for more music and dancing. *"¡Más! ¡Más!"*[38] came a chorus of shouts from around the village square.

"No time for *más,*" Buzz shouted. "Let's get to the helicopter!"

Los dos bailarines y la bailarina[39] scrambled toward the big airship, tossing their costumes into the darkness as they ran. Everyone else was already inside, waiting.

Cincinnati the dancing pig leaped into the pilot's seat, switched on the engine and running lights, and began to spool up the rotors for an immediate departure.

"All present and accounted for, sir!" A saluting Luigi answered Buzz's question before it was even asked.

El sargento García was in the co-pilot's seat. Luigi and Luisa each took window seats on the front row and had a pair of binoculars pressed against the glass. Buzzer Louis and Dusty Louise strapped in next to Luigi and Luisa. And *el mayor Misterioso* and *la señora Kay Tal* sat in the back seats where she began anew, speaking softly, her never-ending report to the major. The big helicopter tilted up in the back and lifted off, turning under Cincinnati's control toward the southeast, and on the trail of the fleeing Fred-X who was headed straight for the *Yucatán*.

Holy *frijoles!*[40]

---

37. all the Primos Indians began to applaud
38. More! More!
39. the two male dancers and the female dancer
40. beans!

* * *

What will happen now? Will the tiny radio transmitters in the gourds work so Fred-X can be followed? Is Fred-X smart enough to figure out he's really stealing a couple of gourds instead of Luigi and Luisa? Will the helicopter have enough fuel to follow Fred-X all the way to the *Yucatán*?

Aprendamos un poco de español

By Dusty Louise

If you are visiting with a Spanish-speaking family, you may need to know how each member is related to all the others. Here are some Spanish words to help you:

parents	los padres	lohs PAH-drehs
mother	la madre	lah MAH-dreh
father	el padre	ehl PAH-dreh
son	el hijo	ehl EE-hoh
daughter	la hija	lah EE-hah
brother	el hermano	ehl air-MAHN-oh
sister	la hermana	lah air-MAHN-ah
grandmother	la abuela	lah ah-BWEH-lah
grandfather	el abuelo	ehl ah-BWEH-loh
grandson	el nieto	ehl nee-EH-toh
granddaughter	la nieta	lah nee-EH-tah
uncle	el tío	ehl TEE-oh
aunt	la tía	lah TEE-ah
niece	la sobrina	lah soh-BREE-nah
nephew	el sobrino	ehl soh-BREE-noh
male cousin	el primo	ehl PREE-moh
female cousin	la prima	lah PREE-mah

* Chapter 10 *

El Señor Luigi— Un Tecnico Muy Excelente[1]

The jet engine whined, then screamed as *el cerdo bailarín* raised the tail of the big helicopter, lifted all three wheels off the ground and swung the big airship in a wide arc around the tall pine tree *en el centro de la aldea*[2] *de los Indios Primos.*

He headed southeast toward *Tampico*[3] where they would have to stop for refueling before leaving land behind and crossing a corner of the Gulf of Mexico toward the *Yucatán*.

"Somebody tune those receivers, please!" Cincinnati the dancing pig was once again in command as captain of the ship. "Let's get a bead on Fred-X as quickly as possible. I sure don't want to overtake him in the darkness and ruin the whole plan," he said to nobody in particular.

El sargento García began flipping toggle switches and turn-

---

1. Mr. Luigi—A Most Excellent Technician
2. in the village's center
3. a city on Mexico's east coast

ing knobs until at first the passengers in *el helicóptero*[4] heard an electronic tone—and then they heard another, the second higher pitched.

"There he is!" Sergeant *García* had found the signals of both the radio transmitters now riding in the hair-covered gourds in Fred-X's clutches. "His heading is one hundred twenty five degrees and he is nine kilometers ahead of us traveling seventy-five kilometers per hour at nine thousand feet," the sergeant reported to Captain Cincinnati.

"Muchas gracias, sargento," Cincinnati spoke into the microphone attached to his headset.

The helicopter was so noisy it would have been too difficult to hear normal conversation without the intercom system. *El cerdo bailarín* corrected their direction to match the radio signals coming from the hairy little gourds in Fred-X's claws, and he slowed the big helicopter to about eighty kilometers per hour as it continued to climb upward.

4. the helicopter

"We'll get within eight kilometers of him and then slow down and maintain our distance," Cincinnati once again spoke almost idly into the little microphone hanging in front of his mouth.

By now all the passengers had put on headsets so they could hear what was being said. Luigi Panettone Giaccomazza and Luisa Manicotti Giaccomazza, being still babies, were so small they had to sit side-by-side and wear only one headset. Their little heads were touching, cheek to cheek, held together by the spring-action tension in the headset, itself.

Luigi was listening with his left ear and Luisa with her right.

Buzzer and Dusty had microphones so they could also join in the conversation.

"Did somebody disconnect *el teléfono de la señorita—la culebra¿*"[5] Dusty Louise spoke into her microphone. "We want to be sure she can't call Fred-X and tell him about the helicopter. Or this *Tal Vez* character, either."

"Sí, sí," sergeant *García* answered. *"La cucaracha* fixed her phone so that no matter what number she dials, it will appear to just ring and ring. Nobody will answer because it is not really ringing anywhere.

"Clever, no¿" he said.

In the back of the big airship, *la señora Kay Tal* was continuing her report to *el mayor Misterioso.* She had punched the bottom out of a large styrofoam coffee cup and placed the smaller bottom of the cup around one of the major's ears. And she was speaking directly into the top of the cup turned mini-megaphone.

5. the young lady's telephone—the snake

"And so, *mi mayor,* once the sheep had crossed *el camino*[6] and we had passed through *la curva de los muertos,*[7] we still had a ways to go to get to the Indian village. Should we stop and rest for a while¿ Or should we continue without stopping¿ That was what we had to decide once we got to the bottom of *el paso de los cráneos.*[8] *¡Ay, ya, ya! ¡Madre de Dios!*[9] So many decisions to be made.

"What would you have done, *mayor¿*" she continued speaking into the makeshift cup-amplifier.

But *el mayor Misterioso* had fallen fast asleep and began to snore so loudly as to almost drown out the whine of the helicopter's jet engine and the pop-pop-pop of the big rotor blades on top.

"Bien. Muy bien. Cuando el mayor duerme, él no es tan estúpido."[10] *La señora Kay Tal* was apparently thinking out loud. Nobody else in the helicopter could have heard what she was saying. Still, she smiled to herself at the thought that the major was the smartest when he was sleeping.

Over the pop-pop-popping of the rotor blades, and the high-pitched whine of the jet engine, everyone could hear the steady hum of the two radio transmitters sending their signals from the gourds covered with the kittens' hair. Those radio signals provided a reassuring drone to the eight adventurers in the helicopter as they trailed the big owl.

Luigi had, by now, removed his half of the headset, making

6. the road
7. dead men's curve
8. skull pass
9. Mother of God!
10. Good. Very good. When the major is asleep, he's not so stupid.

it almost impossible for Luisa to use her half, either. He tapped Buzzer Louis on the shoulder and held up a small card with the words 'Where are we¿' printed on it neatly with a crayon.

Luisa, equally curious, watched intently to see what Buzzer would say.

Buzz leaned over and spoke directly into Luigi's right ear. "We are about halfway between *Ciudad Camargo* and *Tampico*, Luigi," he said. Luigi leaned over and repeated the answer into Luisa's left ear.

She answered him ever so quietly and he shrugged and held up both front paws—questioningly—as if to say, "Beats me."

Luisa began scribbling furiously with her crayon on another card. She held it up for Buzz to see. It said, "What's a *Tampico*¿"

Buzzer motioned for *los gatitos gemelos anaranjados*[11] to put their earphones back on.

"*Tampico*," he began, "is a city on the eastern coast of Mexico. It's a resort city with lots of visitors from around the world every year," he spoke into his little microphone so they could hear him through the earphones.

Now Luigi scribbled madly and held up his card. It said, "Are the visitors all *norteamericanos*¿"

"Good question, Luigi," Buzzer answered into the microphone. "As a matter of fact, most of the visitors come from Europe and Asia. Many of them are Germans and Japanese. And, of course, there's the occasional giant spotted owl with stolen *gatitos norteamericanos*[12] who will drop in from time to time. So to speak," Buzzer winked.

11. the orange kitten twins

12. North American kittens

But the intended humor only seemed to remind Luigi and Luisa that they were both hairless right now. They each pulled a small blanket up to their necks so only their faces were visible.

"The owl's heading more to the east and picking up some speed," Sergeant *García* reported as he watched a radar image of Fred-X on a small screen in front of him. "His heading is now 120 degrees. He's still at 9,000 feet, but his speed has increased to ninety kilometers per hour," the sergeant reported to Cincinnati, who made a slight turn to the left and increased the helicopter's forward speed ever so gently.

"Okay, folks," Cincinnati spoke to everyone through the intercom. "Our old friend, Fred-X, is heading straight for *Tampico*. He'll probably stop there for a few minutes rest, and that'll give us time to refuel our helicopter and still be able to keep up with him."

"How far away are we¿" Dusty wanted to know.

"You see that glow on the horizon straight ahead¿" *el sargento García* answered. *"Allá está la ciudad de Tampico,"*[13] he said to Dusty. "We will be there in *diez o quince minutos."*[14]

"He says the glow on the horizon is *Tampico* and we will be there in ten to fifteen minutes," Dusty translated into the intercom system.

"When we get there," Buzzer said, "I want everybody to jump out of the helicopter while it is refueled. But don't stray—*do not* stray—from the immediate area, please. We'll want to get started again as soon as Fred-X takes off. And if he doesn't stop at all, we really will have to hurry. Do you hear

13. There is the city of Tampico
14. ten or fifteen minutes

me, Luigi and Luisa¿" Buzz concluded with a direct question to *los gatitos gemelos sin pelos.*[15]

"Yes, sir! Stand by close and hop back on board quickly, sir!" It was Luigi, saluting Buzzer as he spoke.

Buzz wasn't sure if Luigi was mocking him or not, so he didn't try to correct the little kitten. After all, Luigi and Luisa had already given all their hair to the cause, so no matter if they were a little silly from time to time.

They were on the team.

In the pilot's seat, Cincinnati spoke into a radio microphone. "*Tampico* Tower, this is whirlybird *X-ray tango alpha tango zebra* from *Ciudad Camargo*, requesting permission to land and asking for refueling urgently. We are on official business for *los federales y el presidente Fox de méjico.*"[16]

"Will they be able to understand you¿" Dusty spoke to Cincinnati. "Do you want me to ask them in Spanish¿" she offered.

"*No es necesario,*[17] Dusty," Cincinnati responded into the intercom. "All air traffic around the world is conducted in English. *?Recuerda bien¿*[18] The controllers at *Tampico* Tower will understand perfectly."

Sure enough, Cincinnati had barely finished his answer to Dusty when the radio crackled and the tower answered, "Whirlybird *X-ray tango alpha tango zebra*, this is *Tampico* Tower, sir. You are cleared to land on helipad two, and the *Pemex* truck is rolling. We will have you refueled in no time, sir."

15. the hairless kitten twins
16. the federales and President Fox of Mexico
17. It's not necessary
18. Do you remember well?

Bright lights suddenly popped on, lighting up the landing pad. Luigi and Luisa, with their binoculars, could see a green and white tanker truck racing to the round, brightly lighted helipad.

Sergeant *García* spoke excitedly into the intercom in rapid-fire Spanish, forgetting that Cincinnati likely could not follow what he was saying at that speed. *"Señor cerdo bailarín, el búho criminal gigante continúa rápidamente. ¡Él no está parando en Tampico!"*[19]

"Más despacio, por favor,"[20] Cincinnati shot back, a worried look on his snout.

"Never mind, sergeant." It was Dusty speaking. "He says Fred-X is not stopping in *Tampico*. He is continuing on toward the *Yucatán* quickly." She finished her translation.

"Then we will have to be even faster in refueling," Buzzer assumed command as the helicopter touched down.

"Everybody out," he said. "Stand by close," he repeated.

As the big airship's rotor blades slowed and began to sag downward, seven of the adventurers climbed quickly to the ground, crouching beneath the still-spinning blades.

A *Pemex* truck rolled to a stop. Its driver jumped out and began pulling a hose to the fuel tank of the helicopter.

"What about *el mayor¿*" *La señora Kay Tal* reminded the others he was still asleep in the back seat. "Should I wake him¿"

"No. Let him sleep. He might decide to direct the refueling, *Kay*," Cincinnati answered decisively.

---

19. Mister dancing pig, the giant criminal owl is going on quickly. He's not stopping in Tampico!

20. More slowly, please

Luigi and Luisa remained wrapped in their little blankets even though it was very warm in *Tampico*. They were still quite self-conscious—even embarrassed—to be seen without their hair.

Los dos hombres de Pemex[21] were giving the helicopter a quick inspection as they filled the fuel tanks. One was inside watching the gauges while the other pumped jet fuel. Although it actually took only about three minutes to refill the tanks, it seemed to Buzzer Louis like an eternity. He worried that Fred-X might slip through their hands if they delayed too long.

"All aboard again," sergeant *García* barked the order as he handed the *Pemex* driver a credit card from *los federales* to pay for the fuel. *"Rápidamente, por favor. ¡Vámosnos!"*[22] he said, waving the small crowd back into the big airship.

Once again Cincinnati fired up the engine, lifted the ship's tail, spun its nose around to the southeast and began to climb rapidly. "Check those radio signals, please, sir." He spoke to *Pablo García*. "Let's see if we can get a fix on our old buddy, Fred-X."

El sargento García at first looked puzzled. Then he looked worried. Just as quickly, he began flipping switches and turning dials. "We have no signals, *capitán*,"[23] he said into the intercom.

"What¿ Not possible!" Buzzer interjected. "We weren't on the ground and out of contact more than three or four minutes. Are you sure you can't find him¿" Buzzer asked.

"I'm working on it, sir, but the receivers are not responding. They seem to be dead!" the sergeant replied.

21. The two Pemex men
22. Quickly, please. Let's go!
23. captain

While everyone else held his or her breath and worried, hairless little Luigi Panettone Giaccomazza decided to take matters into his own paws. He unbuckled his seat belt, hopped quickly down from his seat next to Luisa and scrambled forward and under the instrument panel in the cockpit. It was hard getting there, too, because Captain Cincinnati had the helicopter in a steep climb with its nose pointed upward.

Suddenly one of the radio tones sounded.

Then the other.

"We've got him again!" Sergeant *García* almost shouted. "I don't know how. Five seconds ago, *esta radio estaba muerta*."[24]

"Give me a location, please sir," Cincinnati asked his co-pilot.

"Sixteen kilometers dead ahead and still at 9,000 feet, sir. He has picked up some speed, though. He's zipping along at ninety-five kilometers per hour and headed straight for *Mérida*,"[25] the sergeant responded.

"How did that radio get fixed? *¿Y también dónde en el mundo está Luigi?*"[26] Dusty stared at Luigi's empty seat next to Luisa.

"*No está aquí,*"[27] Luisa attempted a Spanish phrase.

"*Yo estoy aquí.*"[28] Luigi crept out from under the instrument panel, hairless and grinning. "One of the *Pemex* men must have stepped on the radio wires because they were disconnected under here. I fixed them!" Luigi was proud of his contribution.

24. this radio was dead
25. A city on the northern coast of the Yucatán
26. And where in all the world is Luigi?
27. He's not here
28. Here I am.

Buzzer looked puzzled. "I wonder," he spoke softly into the intercom, "if the radio's disconnection was an accident¿

"Or was it sabotage¿"

* * *

What do you think¿ Did the *Pemex* man disconnect the radio on purpose¿ Or maybe was it *el gato gigante negro,*[29] *el mayor Misterioso*¿ After all, he was in the helicopter supposedly sleeping the whole time, wasn't he¿ What might have happened if Luigi hadn't come to the rescue and fixed the radio¿ And what about Fred-X¿ Can he keep going all the way to *Mérida*¿ Is he really so stupid he still doesn't know he's carrying two hairy gourds instead of *los dos gatitos*¿[30]

29. the giant black cat
30. the two kittens

Aprendamos un poco de español

By Dusty Louise

What if you want to talk about sports with someone who speaks only Spanish? How would you say the names of some games? Here are a few to help you:

baseball	béisbol	BAYS-bohl
basketball	baloncesto	bahl-ohn-SESS-toh
cycling	ciclismo	see-CLEES-moh
auto racing	carreras de coches	cah-RARE-ahs deh COH-chehs
skiing	esquí	ehs-SKEE
football	fútbol americano	FOOHT-bohl ah-mare-ee-CAHN-oh
gymnastics	gimnasio	heem-NAH-see-oh
hockey	hockey	OH-kay
running	carrera	cah-REH-rah
sailing	vela	VEH-lah
soccer	fútbol	FOOHT-bohl
swimming	natación	nah-tah-see-OHN
tennis	tenis	TEH-nees
volleyball	vóleibol	VOH-leh-bohl

* Chapter 11 *

La Chocolatada, Reina de Todos Los Gatos Del Yucatán[1]

"Luigi, tú eres un buen técnico—muy excelente,[2] even if you don't have any hair right now," Buzzer Louis complimented the little orange kitten. "You may have just saved the entire expedition by finding and reconnecting those two loose wires, *mi amigo pequeño,"*[3] Buzzer said, proud of his baby brother.

"Gracias, señor,"[4] Luigi responded as he climbed back into his seat and buckled his seat belt snugly. "Everybody just stopped breathing and looked helpless, so I thought somebody ought to do something. The hardest part was climbing uphill to get under the instruments."

Luigi tried desperately—and failed miserably—to seem

1. Chocolate, the queen of all the Yucatan cats
2. Luigi, you are a good technician—very excellent
3. my little friend
4. Thank you, sir

humble as he stared excitedly at the radar screen in front of *el sargento García.*

The two radio signals were strong and unwavering. "Fred-X is continuing south-southeast toward *Mérida*[5] at a steady ninety-five kilometers per hour and still at 9,000 feet," sergeant *García* reported to Captain Cincinnati. "Maybe we should have put a couple of pounds of sand in each of those gourds to slow him down a bit *¿verdad?*"[6] he asked.

"No, no. This is just fine," Cincinnati the dancing pig replied. "We'll burn less fuel at this speed. If we had to go much slower we might not have enough fuel to get across the water to *Mérida,* and I don't particularly fancy the idea of going for a swim tonight," Cincinnati responded to the sergeant.

Luisa, ever curious, held up a small card for Buzzer to see. Printed neatly on it in crayon was the question, "How fast is ninety-five kilometers per hour?"

Buzz motioned for her and Luigi to put on their headset, and then he answered her question. "Let's see, Luisa. If you divide ninety-five by ten, and then multiply by six-point-two-five, we are going, um ... almost sixty miles per hour, I think," Buzzer answered. "That would put us about two hours away from *Mérida.*

"Before you ask, Luisa, *Mérida* is a big city on the northern Gulf coast of Mexico in the state of *Yucatán,*" Buzzer smiled.

Luisa scribbled quickly. Her card said, "Is that where Fred-X takes *todos los gatos mejicanos después de raptarlos?*"[7]

5. A major city in the Yucatán state

6. Right?

7. all the Mexican cats after he steals them?

Dusty Louise, glancing back, was stunned. "Where did you learn that much Spanish¿" Dusty demanded to know.

Luisa scribbled again. *"Cuando usted habla sólo un poco y escucha mucho, usted aprende todo."*[8] She smiled at Dusty—a wry, smug smile of self-satisfaction.

Luigi then scribbled. "Luisa is a lot smarter than she looks, Dusty Louise."

Luisa glowered at Luigi; then she smiled because she knew he meant his comment to be something nice—a compliment.

La señora Kay Tal spoke into the intercom. "*Señor cerdo bailarín,* why is the flight so much smoother now than it was before we got to *Tampico*¿" she asked the captain.

Cincinnati replied, "*Porque estamos sobre el mar, señora.* Flying is almost always smoother *sobre el agua, especialmente durante la noche,*"[9] he explained.

Dusty Louise again looked dumbfounded. How was everyone learning to speak Spanish so easily¿

Sensing her confusion, Buzzer looked over at her and said, "*Tú eres una maestra muy buena,*[10] Dusty Louise."

She smiled at the compliment.

The *gatitos*, confined to their seats for so long, were getting restless.

"Tell us a story, Buzzer. Pleeeease!" Luisa begged.

"Yes, Buzzer. Tell us a story." Luigi chimed in. "Tell us about you and Cincinnati catching bad guys. That would be a fun story, Buzzy. Please."

Realizing he had little else to do for the next hour or so,

8. When you talk only a little and listen a lot, you learn everything.
9. Because we are over the sea, ma'am . . . over water, especially at night
10. You are a very good teacher

Buzzer Louis agreed. "One little story. Just for you, my little *detectives.*"

Buzzer scratched the top of his head, deciding which story of international intrigue to tell the little twins.

"C'mon over here," Buzz said, motioning the kittens over the seat and into his lap. He took off his headset so as not to disturb the others and began to whisper directly into the babies' ears.

"It was five years ago on a dark and stormy night. Interpol—that's the international police agency—had intercepted a wireless phone message from a well-known and very shady Middle Eastern terrorist who was on his way to Rome to assassinate the pope by planting plastic explosives in his little Mercedes 'pope mobile.' The pope mobile was bulletproof, but not plastic explosives-proof, for sure.

"The CIA—Cats-In-Action—called me. Socks ordered me to pick up Cincinnati and go straight to the Vatican to head off the assassin. I was in Denmark at the time, and Cincinnati was in Belgium.

"Pigs seldom venture into Denmark.

"Too often they come out as canned hams.

"I commandeered a NATO supersonic fighter and a pilot, we picked up Cincinnati in Antwerp, and we were in Rome within three hours.

"We reported in to the Swiss Guard at their barracks in Vatican City. They're the group responsible for the pope's safety, you know. Only the Swiss Guard—nobody else—knew that there were, in reality, two identical pope mobiles. Not even the pontiff himself was in on that little secret. So we decided to use one of them as a decoy. And to hide the other in the underground garage at the Vatican radio station."

"What were you and Cincinnati going to do¿" Luisa asked.

"We were introduced first thing in the morning as a pair of famous painters from Latvia who had come to restore the frescoes on the ceiling of the Sistine Chapel, Luisa. It was quite a show, really.

"We were sneaked to the Rome airport—it's called *Fiumicino*—where, on cue, a Vatican limousine picked us up and drove us to St. Peter's Square. There we held a press conference to describe how we would proceed to remove the centuries of dust and grime from some of the world's most famous paintings.

"We were very convincing, I'll tell you that.

"At the end of the press conference, the pope mobile—the one and only as far as anybody knew—picked us up and drove us right into and through the Vatican libraries and museums—smack-dab into the Sistine Chapel, where we began to look very busy with brushes and buckets and little soft-drink-size air compressors. Only thing was, the pope mobile was left right there in the middle of the Chapel. And everybody saw where it was on RAI-1 television in Rome. The press was told that the two of us also would be painting a small mural inside the funny little car as a gift to the pope."

"What happened then, Buzzy¿" Luigi's eyes were big as walnuts.

"Mostly we just looked busy and waited. We knew the terrorist would sneak in at night and put the plastic explosives somewhere in the pope mobile. A radio signal would set it off whenever the pope was next riding in it, and the assassin was ready to strike.

"So we pretended to paint and clean during the daylight, and we hid nearby the pope mobile at night.

"Sure enough, the second night at about three o'clock in the morning a shadowy figure crept into the Sistine Chapel and slithered silently over to the funny looking little Mercedes bubble car. He had the plastics and an explosive-primered, miniature radio receiver in a black metal lunch box.

"Cincinnati and I knew capturing him would be tricky. If he had the triggering transmitter with him, he might just decide to blow us all up—including some of the world's most famous art. We knew we had to trick him.

"Each of us grabbed a paper sack with bread and cheese in it and, on the silent count of three, Cincinnati flipped on all the lights—just as the terrorist was about to open his lunch box filled with destruction.

"Cincinnati said to him, 'Well, hello there. How nice of you to join us. We were just about to step outside for our evening meal. And I see you brought yours, too. We have a jug of wine. C'mon. Go with us.'"

"Did you fool him, Buzzy?" Luisa asked.

"We either fooled him or he was a really cool customer. He just said, 'Thank you. I'd love some company,' and went on outside with us. Of course, we still didn't know if he had the transmitter with him to blow up the lunch box—and us with it."

"Did he eat with you?" Luigi wanted to know.

"Matter of fact, he did. We shared our bread and cheese. But we had a special surprise in the wine—knockout drops. After a couple of sips, he began to get very dizzy and totter about. When he realized he'd been slipped a mickey, he went for the transmitter hidden in his coat pocket."

"What happened? " Luisa looked petrified.

"Well, Luisa, I leaped for the terrorist. And Cincinnati grabbed his lunch box. Then the dancing pig pirouetted twice and flung the lunch box like a discus as far as he could, over the Vatican wall into the service *piazza*[11] where the garbage trucks picked up the Vatican's trash.

"Sure enough, *el terrorista*[12] hit the detonator just as I hit him. There was a huge explosion on the other side of the wall—right inside a dumpster. Well, that dumpster looked like a sardine can that had been run over by a cement mixer truck, but nobody was hurt.

"Cincinnati piled on top of the terrorist and me, and sat on him while I tied him up. By then the Swiss Guards had come to our rescue. They took the bad guy away and locked him up."

"And the pope was saved?" Luisa wanted to be sure.

"The pope was saved. And the little Mercedes pope mobile was saved. Even the paintings in the Sistine Chapel were saved—not only from the terrorist, but also from the two mad painters, Cincinnati the dancing pig and Buzzer Louis, director of operations of the CIA."

"Hooray!" Luigi and Luisa were noisy, happy, relieved and placated.

For the moment.

The kittens' loud cheers pierced through the drone of the jet engine and the flailing of the rotor blades. And woke up *el mayor Misterioso.*

"*¿Dónde estamos ahora?*"[13] he asked sleepily into the intercom. "And have we heard from *la Chocolatada* yet?"

11. Italian word for "plaza." In Spanish, "plaza."
12. the terrorist
13. Where are we now?

"We are over *el golfo de méjico, mayor. ¿Pero, quién es la Chocolatada¿*"[14] Cincinnati answered the half-awake major, curious about this unknown *Chocolatada* character.

"La Chocolatada es la reina de todos los gatos del Yucatán,"[15] the major replied. "I called her this afternoon, and she is expecting us tonight in *Mérida*. She will help us trap *el búho malo,*[16] Fred-X."

Now it was *la señora Kay Tal*'s turn to be dumbfounded. She had no idea the major was capable of doing anything useful on his own.

"Excellent! Wonderful! We'll take all the help we can get," Buzzer slipped into the conversation, still a bit puzzled about what the major was saying. "Is she going to contact us¿" Buzz asked *el mayor.*

Before the major could answer, the helicopter's two-way radio crackled, *"Misión mi primo, misión mi primo. Aquí está la reina de todos los gatos del Yucatán, la Chocolatada. Contéstame, por favor."*[17]

The major smiled.

But Luigi bolted upright, grabbed Buzzer's headset, ripped it off and whispered into Buzz's ear, "How do we know she isn't a friend of Fred-X, Buzzy¿ If it was the major who sabotaged the wires of the radios, maybe he's helping Fred-X. And this *Chocolatada* broad is his moll!" Luigi concluded, throwing both front paws into the air as if signaling a touchdown.

---

14. the Gulf of Mexico. But who is Chocolate?

15. Chocolate is the queen of all the Yucatan cats

16. the bad owl

17. My cousin's mission. The queen of all the Yucatan cats, Chocolate, is here. Answer me, please.

Seeing Luigi's agitation, *el sargento García* spoke into the intercom. "It is *¿Qué quiere decir?* Okay," he said firmly. "*La Chocolatada es la prima del mayor y ella es una gata buena.*[18] You may trust her," he concluded.

Buzzer, understanding more and more Spanish, repeated what the sergeant had said into Luigi's ear and reminded him not to use gangster words such as "broad" and "moll"—words the little kitten had learned by watching old black-and-white Jimmy Cagney movies on The Movie Channel.

Cincinnati, now satisfied that *la Chocolatada* was one of the good guys, grabbed the microphone of the two-way radio and spoke, "*La Chocolatada,* this is whirlybird X-ray tango alpha tango zebra. *Escuchamos tu señal,*"[19] he answered.

Dusty Louise began to wonder if this group really needed an interpreter.

"*Bueno,*" came the response from the radio. "*¿Dónde está?*"[20]

"We are now about forty kilometers northwest of *Mérida* and seven kilometers behind Fred-X, *el búho malo gigante,*"[21] Cincinnati replied. "*¿Dónde está usted?*"[22] he asked.

"*Estoy en el aeropuerto de Mérida.*[23] I will wait here for you to land. I have a taxi standing by. You may be sure Fred-X will land in *Mérida*. I think I have a clue as to where he hides *todos los gatos mejicanos hasta que el señor Tal Vez los mude a Aruba.*"[24]

---

18. How is it said? . . . Chocolate is the major's cousin and she's a good cat
19. We hear your signal
20. Where are you?
21. the big bad owl
22. Where are you?
23. I am at the airport in Mérida.
24. all the Mexican cats until Mr. Tal Vez moves them to Aruba

This time both Buzzer and Cincinnati looked puzzled. Cincinnati mouthed to Dusty, *"No entiendo."*[25]

"She says she thinks she knows where Fred-X may be hiding all the Mexican cats until some guy named *Tal Vez* moves them to Aruba."

"Por favor, dígale que necesitamos dos taxis,"[26] el mayor spoke up.

"Necesitamos dos taxis, por favor,"[27] Cincinnati spoke into the radio microphone.

"No es necesario, capitán," came the reply. *"Aquí conmigo está Tomás, el taxista más rápido de todo el Yucatán. Tiene un taxi muy grande. Un taxi para catorce personas,"*[28] she reported.

Dusty, taking no chances and somewhat protective of her job as interpreter, translated immediately. "She says taxi driver *Tomás* is the fastest driver in all the *Yucatán*, and that his taxi holds fourteen people."

Luigi's eyes bugged out. He looked at Luisa and shouted, "Another limousine. Yahoo!"

"Cincinnati, please tell *la Chocolatada* that we will be there in about *diecisiete minutos*.[29] And ask her, please, not to repeat whatever clues she has about Fred-X's hideout on the radio. One never knows who might be listening in." Buzzer was thinking they ought to play it safe as they closed in on Fred-X and his cat-smuggling gang of dirty crooks.

---

25. I don't understand.

26. Please tell her we need two taxis

27. We need two taxis, please

28. It's not necessary, captain . . . With me here is Thomas, the fastest taxi driver in all the Yucatán. He has a very big taxi. A taxi for fourteen people.

29. seventeen minutes

While Cincinnati was relaying Buzzer's message to *la Chocolatada*, Luisa and Luigi invented yet another new game they called "jump-seat," hopping from the top of one seat to the next, like a couple of precision frogs.

Buzzer motioned for them to sit down and put on their earphones.

"Okay you *two gatitos*," he said. "You have been really good detectives so far on this expedition. Now we're getting close to the capture. I hope, anyway. So I want the two of you to stay right with me after we leave the helicopter. Be my two shadows. Do not stray more than three feet from me. Don't climb any trees. And do not chase any dogs. You will be *mis tropas especiales.*[30]

"*¿Comprende?*"[31]

Luigi stood tall and saluted. *"Sí, sí mi general. Las tropas especiales, a sus órdenes y a su lado,"*[32] he snapped off his salute and—in his exaggerated action—lost his balance and fell headfirst on to the floor of the helicopter.

Luisa laughed. And so did Buzzer. *"Buen muchacho,*[33] Luigi. I knew I could count on you," Buzzer said.

"Fred-X has landed!" Sergeant *García* fairly shouted, pointing out the helicopter's windscreen toward a dark area of the otherwise well-lighted city of *Mérida*. "He is somewhere in that dark area over there. I think it is an old seaport in *Progreso*[34] with warehouses next to the wharf," he reported.

30. my special soldiers
31. Do you understand?
32. Yes, yes my general. The special soldiers, at your service and by your side
33. Good boy
34. A seaport near Mérida

"*Mérida* Tower, this is whirlybird *X-ray tango alpha tango zebra* on official business for *el presidente Fox de méjico* requesting permission to land as closely as possible to the terminal in *ocho minutos,*[35] sir," Cincinnati spoke into the two-way radio's microphone.

"Whirlybird *X-ray tango, alpha tango zebra,* this is *Mérida* Tower. Sir, until 30 seconds ago, we had conflicting traffic. Whatever it was has disappeared off our screens. Did you see any strange, small craft in your area¿" the air traffic controller asked.

"*Mérida* Tower, whirlybird again. Sir, we have been following that small, strange traffic all the way from near *la Ciudad Camargo.* We are aware of it, sir, and you do not, repeat not, need to be concerned. The unidentified craft has landed near the old wharves in *Progreso*, sir.

"Thank you, whirlybird. You are cleared to land immediately at helipad one," the traffic controller responded.

Floodlights popped on suddenly right next to the terminal building. In the edge of the light was another long black Lincoln limousine—this time with a beautiful, long-haired calico cat sitting on the hood.

Cincinnati commented, "There is *el gran taxi*[36] and our new assistant, *la Chocolatada*, ready and waiting. Sergeant, fire up the portable radio receivers and let's get ready to track us down one nasty, mean old owl," Cincinnati issued his last order as helicopter captain while setting the big airship softly in the center of the lighted helipad.

35. eight minutes
36. the big taxi

* * *

Do you think *la Chocolatada,* queen of all the cats of the *Yucatán*, really has any idea where Fred-X is hiding *todos los gatos mejicanos¿* Is her friend, *el taxista Tomás,*[37] really the fastest driver in the whole state¿ Will our merry band of adventurers find all the missing cats, including *Misilusa, la gata sagrada¿*[38] Will Fred-X still be with all the cats¿ Or will he slip away from capture once again¿

37. taxi driver Thomas
38. the sacred cat

Aprendamos un poco de español

By Dusty Louise

If you are ever in a Spanish-speaking country, you will need to know how to describe the weather so you will know what to wear when you go outside. Here are some words that will help you:

weather	*el tiempo*	ehl tee-EHM-poh
climate	*el clima*	ehl CLEE-mah
it is hot	*hace calor*	AH-say cah-LOHR
it is cold	*hace frio*	Ah-say FREE-oh
it is windy	*hay viento*	EYE vee-EHN-toh
rain	*lluvia*	YOO-vee-ah
it is raining	*está lloviendo*	ess-TAH yoh-vee-EHN-doh
rainy	*lluvioso*	yoo-vee-OH-soh
snow	*nieve*	nee-EH-vay
clouds	*nubes*	NOO-behs
storm	*tormenta*	tore-MEHN-tah
thunder	*trueno*	troo-EH-noh
lightning	*relámpago*	reh-LAHM-pah-goh
hail	*granizo*	grah-NEE-soh
temperature	*temperatura*	tehm-pair-ah-TOO-rah
sun	*el sol*	ehl sohl
sunlight	*luz del sol*	loos dell sohl
moon	*la luna*	lah LOO-nah
moonlight	*luz de la luna*	loos day lah LOO-nah

* Chapter 12 *

¡Libertad, Sí! ¡Aruba, No![1]

The beautiful calico *Chocolatada, reina de todos los gatos del Yucatán,*[2] was waiting at the airport in *Mérida* for her cousin Major *Misterioso* and the rest of the adventurers who climbed quickly from the big helicopter.

"Buenas noches, amigos," she greeted them. *"¿Cómo están ustedes?"*[3] she asked.

"We are all fine, but we must hurry," Buzzer responded. "You said on the radio that you had a clue as to the whereabouts of Fred-X's hideout. What do you know about it, please?"

Buzzer felt the need to rush, but also remembered his Hispanic manners—and that rushing, especially when first meeting someone, is considered impolite.

"Sí, sí mi prima. ¿Dónde está el sitio de los gatos?"[4] Major *Misterioso* had awakened from his long nap.

1. Liberty, yes! Aruba, no!
2. Chocolate, queen of all the Yucatan cats
3. Good evening, friends. . . . How are all of you?
4. Yes, yes my cousin. Where is the place with the cats?

"Un momento, primo mio," Chocolatada answered. "First you must meet *el taxista más rápido de todo el Yucatán. Taxista Tomás, aquí están* Buzzer Louis, Dusty Louise, *mi primo—el mayor Misterioso, el sargento García, la señora Kay Tal y el cerdo bailarín* Cincinnati. *Les presento a todos ustedes el taxista Tomás."*[5]

She seemed to be finished with the introductions, and Buzzer was getting impatient to get on with the search even though he understood the need for formalities in a Hispanic country.

"What about us¿" Luigi Panettone Giaccomazza spoke not only for himself, but also for his tiny twin sister, Luisa Manicotti Giaccomazza. "You forgot to introduce us, *Chocolatada*," he reminded her, smiling because he wasn't sure if he was being polite or impertinent.

"¡Ah, sí, sí! Excúsenme, por favor, señor Luigi *y señorita* Luisa. Turning to *el taxista* Tomás, she continued, *"Y también, Tomás, los gatitos gemelos anaranjados,*[6] Luisa *y* Luigi Giaccomazza."

"A sus órdenes,[7] *señor taxista* Tomás," Luisa spoke up—much to Dusty's continuing amazement.

"Now *Chocolatada*, what about this clue as to the whereabouts of all the stolen cats¿" Buzzer pressed to get on with the search.

"El sargento García has a portable radio receiver and we've planted small radio transmitters in some hairy gourds Fred-X brought here, thinking they were Luigi and Luisa," Buzzer blurted out, almost breathlessly.

5. One moment, my cousin. . . . the fastest taxi driver in all the Yucatan. Taxi driver Thomas, here are . . . I present to all of you taxi driver Thomas.

6. Ah, yes, yes. Excuse me, please. . . . And also the orange kitten twins

7. At your service

"*¿Qué?*"[8] *La Chocolatada* looked perplexed.

"There is no time to explain, *Chocolatada*," *el sargento García* stepped into the conversation. "We must get to the old wharves at *Progreso muy pronto*.[15] My *radio portátil*[16] will help us find Fred-X when we get there."

"*Bien. Vámosnos.*[11] Into *el taxi de Tomás, por favor*," *la Chocolatada* finally began to understand the need to hurry. "That is part of the clue I mentioned on the radio, *sargento. Mi otro primo, Santiago de los Campos*,[12] he is—how do you say?—a broker? Yes, a broker of groceries. He tells me that someone is buying large amounts of cat chow and having it delivered to the old wharves at *Progreso*.

"*¿Porqué compra tantos alimentos para los gatos? Yo creo que hay muchos gatos allí.*[13] *¿Verdad?*" she concluded.

To Dusty Louise's continuing amazement, everyone just nodded "yes" as if all of them understood everything *la Chocolatada* had said.

As the long limousine sped away from the airport at *Mérida* and headed at top speed for the wharves at *Progreso*, the two radio signals began to come in to Sergeant *García*'s portable receiver more and more clearly. But it was all he could do to hold onto the radio because *el taxista Tomás* was going so fast.

"*¡Caramba!*[14] This is fun!" Luigi thought going fast was like

---

8. What?
9. very quickly
10. portable radio
11. Good. Let's go.
12. My other cousin, James de los Campos
13. Why buy so much cat food? I think there are lots of cats there.
14. Wow!

icing on the cake of riding again in a big, black Lincoln limousine. He and Luisa resumed their game of jump-seat, sailing back and forth over the heads of the others in the back of the limousine as it flew down the highway.

"Do you know exactly which warehouse the cat food is being taken to¿" Buzzer asked *la Chocolatada*.

"Sí, señor gato tejano.[15] *Es el depósito treinta y nueve.*[16] That is the third warehouse from the south end of the wharves, *yo creo,"*[17] she said with some certainty.

The radio signals became really loud as the big taxi roared, screeching on two wheels into the darkened wharf area at *Progreso*.

"¡Apaga las lámparas, por favor!"[18] Cincinnati, who had said nothing since landing the helicopter at Mérida, suddenly spoke up, asking *el taxista Tomás* to turn out the headlights on the big limo so their approach to *el depósito treinta y nueve* would be more difficult to detect.

"This is the place, all right," *el sargento García* confirmed they were quite near the gourds—the source of the now very loud radio signals.

He switched off the portable receiver.

And the silence suddenly was deafening.

The big limousine, its lights out, pulled silently up to the front door of warehouse thirty-nine. Outside it was really dark—so dark it gave Luigi the chills. "How are we going to do this¿" he whispered to Buzzer.

15. Yes, Mr. Texan cat.
16. warehouse thirty-nine
17. I think
18. Turn out the headlights, please!

"Here's what we'll do now," Buzzer answered. "And, by the way, thank you, *taxista Tomás*, for getting us here so quickly." Buzzer, excited as he was, tried again to remember his manners. "Fred-X knows Cincinnati and me, so we need to stay hidden as long as possible. We will go around to cover the back door. Luigi and Luisa, you two will stay with me. Remember you are *mis tropas especiales.*[19]

"Dusty Louise, you will go with *el sargento García* and *el mayor Misterioso* to the front door. *La señora Kay Tal* and *la Chocolatada* will remain in *el taxi grande con Tomás.*

"When Sergeant *García* shouts '*¡Abra la puerta! ¡Policía!*'[20] then *Tomás*, you turn on the headlights and shine them on the front door. *El sargento García,* Dusty Louise and *el mayor* will break through the front door. And Cincinnati and I will crash through the back door.

"We'll have Fred-X trapped," Buzz said.

"Us too!" Luigi insisted.

"Us too what¿" Buzz asked

"Luisa and I will crash through the back door with you and Cincinnati," Luigi reminded Buzzer. "*Recuerde bien, señor hermano mio. Luisa y yo somos las tropas especiales,*"[21] he concluded.

"Yes, of course, Luigi," Buzzer said. "And will Fred-X be surprised to see you two! He thinks he has brought you all the way from *la aldea de los Indios Primos.*[22] Heh, heh," Buzzer chuckled out loud.

"Okay. *Vámosnos. Danos tres minutos para llegar a la puerta*

19. my special soldiers
20. Open the door! Police!
21. Remember well, mister brother. Luisa and I are the special soldiers
22. the village of the Primos Indians

trasera,[23] and then break through the front, *Pablo.*" Buzzer Louis, retired DO/CIA, gave his last command before departing with the kittens and Cincinnati *a la puerta trasera del depósito treinta y nueve.*[24]

Buzzer and Cincinnati and the kitten twins reached the back door in less than a minute. The wait for *el sargento García*'s signal seemed to take forever.

"What do you think will be in the warehouse¿" Luigi whispered in the darkness.

"I think it may be full of cats and—if we are lucky—Fred-X and this *señor Tal Vez* character from Aruba will also be in there. That way we can end this crime streak all at once," Buzzer whispered back.

The signal, when it came, was loud enough to be heard a mile away. ***"¡Abra la puerta. Policía!"***[25] the sergeant shouted and the sound of wood crashing and splintering was unmistakable.

"*¡Vámosnos!*"[26] Cincinnati gave the command at the back door. Then instead of crashing through the door, he simply reached up and turned the knob and opened it.

"No need to bruise the old picnic ham," he joked. "Let's go get an owl!"

Just as the four of them rushed through the back door, *el mayor* had found the light switches and started turning on the overhead lights. Standing in the middle of the warehouse floor was *un hombre alto y delgado con las manos arriba en el aire.*[27]

---

23. Let's go. Give us three minutes to get to the back door
24. the back door of warehouse thirty-nine.
25. Open the door! Police!
26. Let's go!
27. a tall thin man with his hands high in the air.

"You must be *el señor Tal Vez ¿no?*" *el sargento García* asked the man.

"No hablo inglés, señor. Lo siento. Me llamo Tal Vez de Aruba,"[28] he spoke softly to the sergeant and the major as they handcuffed his wrists behind his back.

"Nosotros lo arrestamos en nombre del presidente Fox y de los federales. Y de todos los gatos de méjico," the sergeant told the swarthy stranger, adding, *"¿Y dónde está tu cómplice,*[29] Fred-X?"

"No está aquí. Él regresa en dos horas, más o menos, señor,"[30] *Tal Vez* answered taking care to be polite and remain calm.

Well, Fred-X may not have been there. But Luigi and Luisa found the cats. Dozens of cats. Hundreds of cats. They crept out of crevice and cranny, perched on the rafters and the windowsills. They came from every corner, from behind every wooden crate. Slowly a chorus of a thousand or more cats began to chant, *"¡Libertad, sí! ¡Aruba, no! ¡Libertad, sí! ¡Aruba, no!"*[31]

"What are they saying, Dusty? Luigi wanted to know.

"They're saying they want to go free, not to Aruba," Dusty Louise answered.

"Look! There is *Misilusa, la gata sagrada!"*[32] Luisa shouted over the din. "We got here in time to save her from being taken to Aruba. Yeah for us!" she set up her own little cheer.

Cincinnati leaned over and whispered something into Buzzer's ear. Buzz nodded, turned to the sergeant and waved

---

28. I don't speak English, sir. I'm sorry. My name is Tal Vez from Aruba

29. We arrest you in the name of President Fox and the federales. And all the cats of Mexico . . . And where is your accomplice

30. He's not here. He returns in two hours, more or less, sir

31. Liberty, yes! Aruba, no!

32. the sacred cat!

a paw twice. Seeing the prearranged signal from Buzzer, *el sargento García* hopped onto a wooden crate, raised his hands above his head and shouted, ***"¡Silencio, por favor. Silencio, gatos!"***[33]

The chanting slowly wound down. Sergeant *García* spoke to the assembled cats in a reassuring tone. "You will all be taken home by tomorrow at this time," he told all the cats who—by now—had moved toward the center of the warehouse floor and looked for all the world like a giant, living carpet. "But right now we need to get you out of here. *Mi compadre,*[34] *la señora Kay Tal,* has called for *dos autobuses*[35] to take you all to the *Mérida* Hilton where you will be the overnight guests of *los federales."*

He raised both his arms in the air and shook his clenched fists as the assembled cats began to cheer.

"Ahora, por favor,"[36] he continued, "be quiet and follow *el mayor* here out the back door. Pretend this is a fire drill at school. No talking. Stay in line, please. We will get you on one of the buses to the hotel *muy pronto."*[37] The sergeant hopped down, walked up to Buzzer, smiled and said, "Was that okay¿"

"Perfecto, sargento,"[38] Buzzer answered as the cats made their way—quietly and orderly— out the back door to the waiting buses.

Once they had all cleared the back door and Cincinnati had

33. Quiet, please. Quiet, cats!
34. My friend
35. two buses
36. Now, please
37. very quickly
38. Perfect, sergeant

shut it again, Buzz spoke, "Now we have two hours, maybe less, to get ready for Fred-X. Dusty, turn out all the lights except this one little one over here, please. Sergeant, ask *el taxista Tomás que maneje el gran taxi*[39] into the warehouse—and to bring in with him a *la señora Kay Tal* and her laptop computer," Buzzer continued giving directions.

* * *

What is Buzzer Louis up to? Do you think they will all be ready when Fred-X returns? Will they be able to capture him as easily as they captured the shady smuggler?

39. to drive the big taxi

Aprendamos un poco de español

By Dusty Louise

When you eat a meal in a Spanish-speaking country, you will need to know what to call things on the table. Here are a few words to help you get ready to eat:

table	*la mesa*	lah MACE-ah
chair	*la silla*	lah SEE-yah
dining room	*el comedor*	ehl coh-may-DOHR
kitchen	*la cocina*	lah coh-SEE-nah
plate	*el plato*	ehl PLAH-toh
cup	*la taza*	lah TAH-sah
glass	*el vaso*	ehl VAH-soh
knife	*el cuchillo*	ehl coo-CHEE-yoh
fork	*el tenedor*	ehl ten-eh-DOOR
spoon	*la cuchara*	lah coo-CHAR-ah
napkin	*la servilleta*	lah sair-vee-YATE-ah
bowl	*el tazón*	ehl tah-SOHN
tablecloth	*el mantel*	ehl mahn-TELL

* Chapter 13 *
La Gran Sorpresa Final[1]

The inside of warehouse thirty-nine at the wharves at *Progreso* was as dark as the bottom of a coal bin. Only the glow from the screen of *la señora Kay Tal*'s computer, and from one carriage light inside the back of *el taxista Tomás*'s big Lincoln limousine, made it possible to see at all.

"Hold still please, *mayor.*" *La señora Kay Tal* worked in the back of the limousine, studying the computer screen filled with Buzzer Louis's portrait, which Buford Lewis and Bogart-BOGART had sent by e-mail. She was applying some kind of pasty white substance to the face and neck of the major while Luigi Panettone Giaccomazza and Luisa Manicotti Giaccomazza looked on.

"A little more under the chin, *señora,*" Luigi suggested.

"And don't forget the black goatee," Luisa added.

Meanwhile Buzzer and his long-time friend Cincinnati *el cerdo bailarín* were talking in a dark corner of the warehouse on

1. The Last Big Surprise

Buzz's little satellite phone. They spoke with Buford Lewis and Bogart-BOGART back at *la hacienda pequeña en las colinas de tejas.*[2]

"And so, Buford and Bogart-BOGART, *la cucaracha's* plan worked perfectly," Buzzer said into the *teléfono pequeño.*[3] "We tracked Fred-X right to the warehouse where he kept *todos los gatos méjicanos.*[4]

"All the cats have been set free, including *Misilusa, la gata sagrada de los Indios Primos*. The *federales* will take them all back to their rightful homes tomorrow. And *el señor Tal Vez* is in the calaboose.

"Or as they say here in *méjico, 'Él está en la cárcel.'*"[5]

"Great, Buzzer! What about Fred-X¿ Will you be able to capture him¿" Buford Lewis wanted to know.

"We're getting ready right now, Buford, for *la gran sorpresa final,*" Cincinnati responded to Buford's question. "This is the big surprise for Fred-X that we needed Buzzer's portrait to set up."

"Let me guess! Let me guess!" Bogart-BOGART wanted to try to figure out how the big trap for Fred-X would work.

"Okay Bogart-BOGART. How do you think we'll surprise Fred-X¿" Buzzer decided to let Buford's very smart brother try to unscramble the puzzle.

"First," Bogart-BOGART said, "*el mayor Misterioso* is a giant black cat. The biggest black cat you have ever seen. *?Verdad¿* Buzzer."

"That's right, Bogart-BOGART," Buzzer answered.

---

2. the little ranch in the Texas hills
3. small telephone
4. all the Mexican cats
5. He is in jail.

"In fact," Bogart-BOGART continued, "he may be eight or ten times as big as you, Buzz. Right¿"

"Correcto, también,"[6] Cincinnati answered this time, starting to anticipate the accuracy of Bogart-BOGART's logic.

"Second," the very smart brother of Buford Lewis went on, "the one thing in the world that Fred-X is most afraid of is . . . Is what¿

"Buzzer Louis. That's what!" He answered his own question, not waiting for any reaction from his *compadres*[7] in Mexico.

"Right, again, Bogart-BOGART," Buzzer affirmed. The big dog was getting close to the right answer, for sure.

"So," Bogart-BOGART continued to solve the puzzle. "What if Fred-X were to be surprised by a Buzzer Louis who weighed a hundred pounds—instead of the twelve pounds he's already so afraid of¿ Heh, heh, heh," he snickered at his own cleverness. "Am I right, Buzzer¿" Bogart-BOGART asked, knowing for sure he had nailed the plan.

Dead-on.

"Usted está correcto, señor. Cincinnati, *mándele al Bogart-BOGART un gran cigarro cubano,"*[8] Buzzer congratulated Bogart-BOGART for figuring out their very clever plan.

"La señora Kay Tal is right now using my portrait from her computer screen, along with a bottle of flour paste, to make *el mayor* look exactly like a giant version of me," Buzzer said. "In the dark, a hundred pound Buzzer Louis ought to scare all the meanness out of Fred-X. Once and for all time.

"Of course," Buzz continued, "I will be doing the talking.

6. Right, again
7. friends
8. You are right, sir. . . . send Bogart-BOGART a big Cuban cigar

The major will simply open and close his mouth as if he were speaking ... instead of me. Do you like the plan, Buford Lewis¿" Buzzer asked.

"Truly diabolical, Buzzer! My hat's off to you for being so clever and creative. I hope it works and scares Fred-X so much that he never wants to see another cat again," Buford said.

"Now go get ready for him, Buzzer and Cincinnati. And call us when Fred-X is tucked away neatly in the hoosegow. Okay¿" Buford said as he clicked off the connection.

Dusty crept up just as Buzzer put his little phone away. "You want to see how it's coming along¿" she asked Buzz and Cincinnati. "You're looking pretty scary at eight times your normal size, I must say. Heh, heh, heh," she snickered.

Dusty, Buzzer and Cincinnati tiptoed carefully in the darkness toward the tiny glowing light coming from the backseat *el gran taxi del taxista Tomás en el centro del depósito treinta y nueve.*[9]

Peering into the backseat of the big Lincoln, Buzzer gave a gasp and recoiled, while Cincinnati began to laugh hysterically, thinking of the coming reaction from *el gigantesco búho criminal.*[10] They were looking straight on at what Fred-X would no doubt perceive to be a huge Buzzer Louis.

In addition to the paste makeup helping the major look just like Buzzer, *el sargento García* had placed the hairy, Luigi-and-Luisa-look-alike gourds in the big black cat's front paws. The major looked like a hundred pound version of Buzzer Louis, protectively cradling *los gatitos gemelos anaranjados*.[11]

---

9. taxi driver Thomas's big taxi in the middle of warehouse thirty-nine
10. the giant criminal owl
11. the orange kitten twins

Luigi and Luisa halted their game of frog-like precision jump-seat long enough to check out the progress. "Boy, that Fred-X is going to be surprised. Ha, ha, ha," Luigi spoke the obvious with a huge smile on his tiny face.

"May we say something to him, too, Buzzer¿" Luisa raised one eyebrow and asked to be included in the action.

"Since we've taken all your hair, I believe you two may say whatever you want to Fred-X," Buzz answered. "Just don't give away the secret, please. Let him believe these ridiculous gourds actually are talking to him. *¿Comprende¿*"[12] Buzzer asked.

"Sí, sí mi hermano gato más grande de todo el mundo."[13] Luigi stood tall and saluted yet once again—almost tripping but catching his balance—this time at the last minute.

Excited at the prospect of getting even with Fred-X, Luisa and Luigi resumed their fascinating game of precision jump-seat, from time to time enhancing the action by making the croaking noises of frogs with each leap. "Ribbit. Rib-bit. Rib-bit." What fun!

"El trabajo es muy bueno, señora."[14] Buzzer motioned to the major's face as he complimented *Kay Tal* on the makeup application. She nodded her thanks from the dark limousine's backseat.

"Sí, sí. La apariencia es muy salvaje.[15] *Ja, ja, ja,"* Cincinnati was still snickering to himself.

"Look at the time, Buzzy," Dusty Louise said quickly and with some alarm in her voice. *"Las dos horas*[16] are about up,"

12. Understand?
13. Yes, yes my brother cat, the biggest in all the world.
14. It's a very good job, madam.
15. Yes, yes. The appearance is very wild.
16. The two hours

she continued. "Shouldn't we be getting ready for Fred-X to meet the monster cat¿" She, too, snickered, putting both front paws in front of her face to keep from laughing out loud.

"Lo siento,"[17] she added quickly, apologizing for not being able to keep a straight face. "It's just so hard to be serious when I think about what will happen when Fred-X sees *el gato blanco y negro más gigantesco del mundo."*[18] Again, she broke into a snicker and covered her mouth with both front paws.

"Right, Dusty!" Buzzer assumed command and tried to be serious once again. "Let's get ready. And let's start by ending for now this game of jump-seat, you two little *ranas imaginarias."*[19] He spoke directly to Luigi and Luisa, smiling at their antics and glad to see them having some fun in spite of their pitiful, hairless state.

"Everybody take your places," Buzzer continued.

"*Sargento Pablo,* you will hide in the darkness and pretend you are *el señor Tal Vez de Aruba.* You will tell Fred-X to get into the fine big, black limousine you have bought for him with your catnapping profits. Open the door for him, give him a little shove and slam the door behind him. *?Listo, señor¿"*[20] Buzzer finished his instructions to the *federal* sergeant.

"Now *señora Kay Tal, usted, la Chocolatada y* Dusty Louise[21] will also hide in the dark in different places around the warehouse. Continue to meow like cats. Make yourselves sound like dozens of cats. Hundreds of cats. Can you do that¿"

17. I'm sorry
18. the biggest black-and-white cat in the world
19. imaginary frogs
20. Ready, sir?
21. you, Chocolate and Dusty Louise

Buzzer asked, not expecting an answer and adding, *"Muy bien y gracias, mis amigas."*[22]

"Taxista Tomás, cuando el búho criminal gigantesco[23] gets into the backseat, you will turn on the corner carriage light to shine on the face *del mayor,* aka Buzzer Louis. Then lock all the doors with the electric lock, *por favor. ¿Está bien, señor?"*[24] Buzzer questioned taxi-driver Thomas who nodded an emphatic "yes."

"Luisa and Luigi, the two of you will each hide under one of the little fold-down seats in front of the major. You may speak whenever and whatever you like. As you speak, *el mayor* will wiggle one or the other of the hairy little gourds—as if your voices were coming from them. Ho, ho, ha, ha, hee, hee!"

Buzzer had lost his serious manner and began to laugh out loud thinking about the wiggling, talking and hairy little gourds—and knowing Luigi and Luisa were liable to say anything, but surely something very funny. Whatever popped into their tiny, hairless little heads, most likely.

Cincinnati the dancing pig, still snickering and trying not to laugh out loud, asked Buzzer, "What would you like me to do, Buzzy?"

"How about if you hide in the middle seat, then jump over to the back and do a little song and dance like you did in front of the Holiday Inn back in *la Ciudad Camargo?* Remember, though, Fred-X is almost as afraid of you as he is of me. Then you can help us hold him down while *el sargento García* restrains him and gets him ready for his new home—a padded cell."

22. Very good, and thanks, my friends.
23. when the giant criminal owl
24. please. Right, sir?

Buzzer snickered again at the thought, but was able not to laugh out loud this time.

He continued, "I will hide *en el baúl y le hablaré a*[25] Fred-X from there while you, *mayor*, move your mouth open and closed as if you were doing the talking." Buzzer concluded his instructions to all the adventurers.

"*¿Todos listos?*"[26] Buzz asked, more as a final signal for all to take their places than as a question.

"Somebody's coming!" It was Dusty Louise who sounded the warning just as the front door—which Sergeant *García* had fixed after crashing through it earlier—was pushed open about two feet and a giant shadow fell across the inside of *el depósito treinta y nueve,*[27] cast by the now bright moonlight outside.

* * *

Is it Fred-X? Will our merry band be able not to laugh long enough to finally trap *el búho criminal gigante* and put an end to his catnapping ways once and for all? What in the world do you think Luigi and Luisa might say to Fred-X once he's locked inside the big black taxi?

25. in the trunk and speak to
26. Everybody ready?
27. warehouse thirty-nine

Aprendamos un poco de español

By Dusty Louise

In everyday conversation, you may wish to know how to respond to those speaking Spanish. Here are a few words and phrases to help you through almost any conversation:

Thank you	*gracias*	GRAH-see-ahs
you're welcome	*de nada*	deh NAH-dah
Hello (as in answering phone)	*¡Pronto!*	PROHN-toh
goodbye	*adios*	ah-dee-OHS
good/well	*bien*	bee-EHN
very good	*muy bien*	MOO-ey bee-EHN
please	*por favor*	pohr fah-VOHR
at your service	*a sus órdenes*	ah soos OHR-deh-nehs
I want to introduce you to	*quiero presentarle*	kee-AIR-oh preh-sen-TAHR-leh
sir	*señor*	sane-YOHR
ma'am	*señora*	sane-YOHR-ah
miss	*señorita*	sane-yohr-EE-tah
what time is it?	*¿Qué hora es?*	kay OHR-ah ess
where are we going?	*¿A dónde vamos?*	ah DOHN-deh VAH-mohs
ready?	*¿Listo?*	LEE-stoh
let's go	*vámosnos*	VAH-mohs-nohs
okay/good/sure	*bueno*	BWAIN-oh
more slowly	*más despacio*	MAHS dehs PAHS-yoh
How's it going?	*¿Qué tal?*	kay TAHL
maybe	*tal vez*	tahl VASE

* Chapter 14 *

Gracias a Los Cuatro Gatos Amigos Tejanos[1]

Following completion of their work in *Mérida, los cuatro gatos tejanos* and Cincinnati the dancing pig were picked up by the president of Mexico's private airplane and flown directly to Mexico City. There they were to be honored with a big ceremony.

Luigi thought the president's plane was not quite as nice as Cincinnati's *The Flying Pig Machine*—although it was much larger—and he was not happy that the uniformed, white-gloved steward refused to let him and Luisa play jump-seat during the flight.

"After all," he said to Buzzer, "we are heroes, aren't we¿"

When they arrived in Mexico City, flags were waving crazily everywhere in a light breeze on the square in front of the presidential palace. Red, white and blue flags of the United States; red, white and green flags of the Republic of Mexico; and red, white and blue flags of the lone star state of Texas.

1. Thanks to the Four Texan Cat Friends

Thousands of adoring fans and well-wishers had already gathered, and the crowd was growing by the minute. Television crews were setting up their equipment in an attempt to get a good shot of the heroes of the day in Mexico, *los cuatro gatos tejanos* and their friend Cincinnati the dancing pig.

Upstairs at the palace, in the president's private library, Buzzer Louis was on his digital satellite telephone telling Buford Lewis, Ph.D. and his very smart brother Bogart-BOGART exactly what had happened when Fred-X returned to warehouse thirty-nine on the docks of *Progreso*.

"We were all in place and ready when the door opened and the unmistakable shadow of that evil owl, Fred-X, spilled into the warehouse," Buzzer began his account.

"*La señora Kay Tal*, Dusty Louise and *la Chocolatada—reina de todos los gatos del Yucatán*—began to meow and howl from different corners of the big room. Because the warehouse was almost totally empty, their cries echoed and bounced around inside, making them sound like hundreds of cats. It was quite a raucous noise, I'll tell you, Buford and Bogart-BOGART," Buzzer continued.

"What happened then¿" Bogart-BOGART was anxious to know.

"Well, Bogart-BOGART, as Fred-X walked into the warehouse, *el sargento García* hid in the darkness and began to pretend to be *el señor Tal Vez de Aruba*. He said to Fred-X, 'Welcome back, my winged friend. *Venga aquí, pronto. Vea lo que compré para usted, amigo mio—una limosina grande y nueva. ¡Mire! ¡Mire usted, amigo mio!*'"[2]

"Did Fred-X fall for it¿" Buford Lewis was anxious.

"Oh, you bet, Buford. He fell for it all right. He rushed right up to the shiny black limo and smiled the greediest smile you ever saw."

"Then what happened¿" Bogart-BOGART was getting ever more impatient to get to the action.

"I'll try to tell you exactly what happened without laughing," Buzzer Louis responded, "but sometimes it gets pretty funny. So bear with me, *por favor, amigos*.

"*El sargento García* reached out of the darkness and opened the fourth back door on the left a crack, inviting *el búho criminal gigante* to get into 'his' new limo. *'Entre usted, amigo. Siéntese en los asientos finos de cuero, suaves como un sofá,'*[3] *el sargento* said to Fred-X, disguising his voice to sound like *el señor Tal Vez,"* Buzzer continued.

"Did he get in¿" Buford asked.

"Oh, yes, Buford Lewis, Fred-X hopped right in. *El sargento*

---

2. Come here, quickly. Look at what I have bought for you, my friend—a new, big limousine. Look. Look my friend!

3. Get in, friend. Sit on the fine leather seats, soft as a sofa

García slammed shut the door, and then *el taxista Tomás* locked the doors and turned on one pin-light in the backseat.

"And then the fun began, I can tell you that," Buzzer chuckled.

"Tell us what happened!" Bogart-BOGART was sounding even more urgent, wanting desperately to get to the capture of Fred-X.

Buzzer continued. "Just as the light came on to shine on *el mayor's* face, Fred-X looked up, gulped, froze and stared. He tried to say something but only 'aaarrrgh' came out of his mouth.

"Then as the major moved his mouth, I said from my hiding place in the trunk, 'You are dead-meat, Fred-X. I've grown since you last saw me in the Hill Country and I am about to teach you a lesson.'

"Fred-X's eyes just kept getting wider and wider. I thought his eyeballs might fall out of their sockets. 'You! Cat!' he sputtered. 'You have followed me and you have tricked me once again.'

'"Right, Fred-X,' I said as the major opened and closed his huge mouth, reflecting the pin light off his teeth and back onto Fred-X in flashes, like miniature strobe lights. 'We are going to put you away for a long, long time,' I said.

"Just then Luigi piped up," Buzz continued, "and the major wiggled one of the hairy gourds to make it look like it was Luigi speaking. 'The judge and jury at your trial will all be cats, *búho malvado,* and the warden and all the guards at your prison will all be cats, too. Heh, heh, heh,' he finished with a sinister laugh."

Buford and Bogart-BOGART paid rapt attention as Buzzer

went on with his account. "Luisa then added as the major wiggled the other gourd, 'You wanted cats. You're going to get cats, Mr. Meanie Owl. You won't see another living soul but cats for the next, oh, say ten or fifteen years. Ha, ha, ha.' Her laugh was even more sinister sounding than Luigi's.

"Fred-X was sputtering and trying to see a way out of his predicament when Cincinnati the dancing pig commenced, from his hiding place in the middle seat, to moan a soulful cry. He launched into a an eerie blues song he had learned on Beale Street in Memphis. Amidst the singing, he leaped over the seat, landed in front of Fred-X and began a slow, herky-jerky dance in time to the sad song he was singing," Buzzer continued.

"We all started to laugh because Fred-X looked so amazed. He jumped away from Cincinnati, banging into the side of the car and shouting, 'Oh, no! The Ohio dancing pig! This is too much. I give up!'

"And then he fainted. Just fell into a heap of feathers in the back floor of the big Lincoln," Buzzer went on with his story for Buford Lewis and Bogart-BOGART.

"What did you do then¿" Buford wanted to know.

"Well, Buford, Cincinnati screamed 'Banzai!'—why he chose that particular exclamation, I don't know—and jumped right on top of Fred-X, pinning him to the floor of the limo. *El taxista Tomás* unlocked the doors and *el sargento García* climbed in and put wingcuffs on Fred-X. Leg shackles, too, locking him to the back door handle.

"Then everybody jumped into the middle seat and Tomás, *el taxista más rápido del Yucatán,* took off like a bullet and lit out for the jail in *Mérida*. And that's where Fred-X is right now—

three cells down from his old partner, *el señor Tal Vez de Aruba,"* Buzzer concluded the retelling of the capture of *el búho criminal gigantesco*.

"Great work, Buzzer!" Buford was genuinely proud of his cat friends. "When will y'all be coming home¿" he asked.

"Probably tomorrow, Buford," Buzzer answered. "We have to join *el presidente Fox de méjico* pretty soon for a special presentation on the balcony of the presidential palace overlooking a huge square. They tell us that will happen in a few minutes. Turn on CNN World News, and maybe you'll see us.

"Then we'll have to answer questions from the press and—this afternoon—go back to *Ciudad Camargo* to retrieve *The Flying Pig Machine.* The *federales* offered to fly it here for Cincinnati, but he decided we should go get it ourselves. He said nobody but him had ever flown the craft and he preferred to keep it that way.

"So I think we'll probably be home about midday tomorrow," Buzzer said as he bid his canine friends back at the little ranch 'goodbye' and closed the cover on his telephone.

Just as he finished his conversation with the ranch, *la señora Locutora*—the tall lady dressed all in black who had started the whole adventure with her visit to *la hacienda pequeña en las colinas de tejas*[4]—came bustling into the room holding another card in front of her. She put on her reading glasses and spoke. *"Buenos días, Cincinnati y mis amigos tejanos."*[5]

Catching her mistake and not knowing that the Texans all could now understand a lot of Spanish, she quickly shifted to reading in English. "In a few minutes, *el presidente Fox* will join you and you will all go out onto *el balcón*—the balcony—

4. the little ranch in the hills of Texas
5. Good morning, Cincinnati and my Texas friends

where you will be greeted by a large crowd of grateful *meji-canos," la señora Locutora* told the somewhat nervous group of adventurers.

"Then *el presidente Fox* will award each of you *El Premio Distinguido de Los Ciudadanos de Méjico, la medalla más preciosa de nuestro país,"*[6] she once again mistakenly reverted to Spanish, but by now everyone could understand.

Mostly, anyway.

"In view of your *sacrificio muy grande de sus pelos,*[7] Luigi Panettone Giaccomazza and Luisa Manicotti Giaccomazza, *el presidente* wants to give you something extra. He will ask you what you want. Please think about it and be prepared to answer him, okay¿" *La señora Locutora* concluded her instructions just as the president walked briskly into the room and motioned, smiling, for the group to join him on *el balcón*.

"Wow, Luisa! Anything we want. Holy *frijoles*!" Luigi whispered to his twin sister.

"Don't be greedy, Luigi," Luisa cautioned softly as everyone was ushered onto the balcony to the roar of an adoring and grateful crowd in *la plaza* below.

When the roar of the crowd died down a bit, the president spoke into a microphone. *"Los cuatro gatos tejanos y su amigo Cincinnati el cerdo bailarín, tengo mucho gusto en presentarles el premio más distinguido de todos los ciudadanos de méjico con un gigantesco 'gracias.' Gracias amigos norteamericanos,"*[8] he concluded as

6. The Distinguished Medal of the People of Mexico, the most valuable medal of our country

7. the very great sacrifice of your hair

8. I am happy to present to you the most distinguished medal of all the people of Mexico with a giant 'thank you.' Thank you my North American friends

he handed each of the adventurers a small leather case lined with velvet and containing a beautiful silver medal.

"Y ahora," el presidente Fox continued, *"algo especialmento pequeño para los gatitos gemelos anaranjados, Luigi y Luisa. ¿Qué desea, Luisa¿"*[9]

The huge crowd below held its breath as Luisa stepped to the microphone and began to speak in her tiny kitten voice, *"Yo quiero sólo un pañolón pequeño, señor."*[10]

The crowd roared its approval as Luisa turned to Luigi and said softly, "Just to keep me warm until my hair grows back out."

---

9. And now . . . a little something for the twin orange kittens, Luigi and Luisa. What would you like, Luisa?

10. I would only like a small shawl

El presidente stepped back to the microphone. *"¿Y usted, Luigi? ¿Qué desea, mi gatito amigo?"*[11]

Luisa was pretty sure Luigi would ask for a long, shiny black Lincoln limousine as he stepped to the microphone. Luigi began his answer. *"Señor, yo quiero un paquete gigante de cacahuetes con sal, por favor. Tengo mucha hambre."*[12]

The crowd went wild, screaming their approval of Luigi's special request. *El presidente Fox* smiled—relieved, no doubt, that Luigi did not ask for a big airplane or something else very expensive.

"Una cosa más," el presidente said into the microphone. *"En nombre de todos los gatos de méjico—no, de todos los gatos del mundo—le presento a usted, señor Buzzer Louis, un cheque de un milion de pesos del Banco de Mejico. ¡Gracias a usted también, señor!"*[13]

As the crowd below continued to shout out their gratitude, Buzzer, Dusty, Luigi, Luisa and Cincinnati all waved, smiled, and backed slowly from the balcony into the president's library.

"If I had a special wish," Dusty Louise said softly to Cincinnati, "I would just ask to go home. I'm very tired."

El presidente Fox must have overheard Dusty. He turned to her, leaned down and said, "We will arrange for all of you to travel immediately to *Ciudad Camargo, señorita* Dusty. From there you may fly directly home in the airplane of the dancing pig. I am told you are learning to fly it, *también. Eso es bueno, señorita. Muy bueno,"*[14] he said with a smile.

---

11. And you, Luigi? What would you like, my little kitten friend?

12. I want a giant package of salted peanuts, please. I am very hungry.

13. One more thing. . . . In the name of all Mexican cats—no, all the world's cats—I present to you a check for one million pesos from the Bank of Mexico. Thanks again, sir!

14. That's good, miss. Very good

* * *

What will happen now? Will Luigi get his giant bag of salted peanuts? Will Luisa get her shawl? What will Buzzer Louis do with the check for a million pesos?

Aprendamos un poco de español

By Dusty Louise

Here is a recap of some useful, simple phrases to help you have a conversation in Spanish:

Hello	hola	OH-lah
How are you?	¿Cómo está usted?	COH-moh ess-TAH oo-STED
What is your name?	¿Cómo se llama?	COH-moh say YAH-mah
My name is Dusty	Me llamo Dusty	may YAH-moh Dusty
Thank you	gracias	GRAH-see-ahs
you're welcome	de nada	day NAH-dah
good morning/day	buenos días	BWAIN-ohs DEE-ahs
good afternoon	buenas tardes	BWAIN-ahs TAHR-des
good evening/night	buenas noches	BWAIN-ahs NOH-ches
goodbye	adiós	ah-dee-OHS
What time is it?	¿Qué hora es?	kay OHR-ah ESS
please	por favor	pohr fah-VOHR
I don't speak Spanish	no hablo español	noh AH-bloh ess-pahn-YOHL
Speak more slowly	hable más despacio	AH-blay mahs dehs-PAH-syoh
I'm hungry	tengo hambre	TEN-goh AHM-breh
Glad to meet you	mucho gusto	MOO-choh GOO-stoh

* Epilogue *
En La Casa de Las Colinas, Otra Vez[1]

Several days after returning from their big Mexican adventure, the whole experience was beginning to seem like a dream to *los cuatro gatos tejanos* and their friend Cincinnati the dancing pig. The flight home from Ciudad Camargo to the Hill Country Intergalactic Airport had been mostly uneventful.

Restful, even.

Along the way, Buzzer had produced a little bottle of what he called "magic potion" he claimed was given to him by *la cucaracha.* "It's to make your hair grow back faster," he told Luigi and Luisa as he rubbed drop after drop onto their prickly skin. "*La Cucaracha* told me it has an eighty-four percent success rate in clinical tests," he smiled at the hopeful kitten twins.

Cincinnati had noticed the shape of the bottle and its label that looked to him suspiciously like something he had seen on television from an outfit called *The Hair Club for Animals and*

1. At Home Again in the Hills

Other Balding Quadrupeds, but—given its enthusiastic application by Buzzer and its hoped-for results from Luigi and Luisa, he kept the little secret information to himself.

"Just my luck I'll be in the sixteen percent that failed," Luisa commented, holding her nose at the somewhat foul-smelling liquid Buzzer was dropping onto her and rubbing into her skin.

"Don't be so negative, Luisa," Luigi had countered. "Remember, we must have been pretty lucky just to have been able to go on this adventure, capture Fred-X and get big silver medals from *el presidente Fox.* This stuff's going to work," he said to his sister. "Not to mention the peanuts. And your shawl."

Another classic shift of subject matter from Luigi, the master of changespeak.

"Please don't," Luisa responded. "Mention them, that is. I wish I had asked for one of those beautiful embroidered white dresses like Dusty was wearing at the St. Swithen's Day festival. In a couple of weeks I'm not going to even need this shawl—if that stuff Buzzer's spreading around even works at all."

She sighed at missed opportunities.

Luigi, on the other hand, was perfectly happy with his *cacahuetes con sal,*[2] although Cincinnati was not too keen on the mess the little kitten was making, cracking and eating them in the formerly immaculately clean *The Flying Pig Machine.*

Luisa smiled at Luigi and they started back to their seemingly never-ending game of precision jump-seat. Unlike the steward aboard the president's big jet, Cincinnati and his

2. salted peanuts

second in command, co-pilot Dusty Louise, allowed the little scamps to jump and play. As long as the air at 33,000 feet was smooth. And the two were in no danger of hurting themselves.

Or someone else.

After they had returned to the Hill Country, Cincinnati had stayed on at the little ranch for several days to finalize plans for his new dance studio on Main Street—Cincinnati Number 114. Construction plans were ready, thanks to some fast work by his assistant, Bonzo. Bob the troll had agreed to manage the enterprise for *High-Steppin' Pigs, LLC*—Cincinnati's far-flung holding company.

After piloting *The Flying Pig Machine* most of the way back from Mexico, a very enthusiastic Dusty Louise had promptly enrolled in flying lessons at the HCIA pilot's lounge. She secretly hoped she could talk Buzzer into spending his one million *pesos*[3] reward on a decent airplane.

She had started dropping not-too-subtle hints on the subject from time to time.

Buford Lewis, Ph.D. and his very smart brother Bogart-BOGART were just happy to have some real friends back at the ranch to talk to in person. Long distance phone updates were okay, they said, but much too limited. "You need to get a pair of those new photo phones, Buzzer," Buford said, "so we could see the expressions on your faces and read your body language."

"Face-to-face conversation just can't be beat—at least not for the less than five thousand *pesos* it would take to get a pair of those little babies," Bogart-BOGART said.

3. Mexican "dollar." Worth about a dime.

Seemed everybody had designs on some of the million *pesos* Buzzer had been carrying around in his pocket.

And, speaking of those million *pesos* ... when Buzzer Louis went to the local branch of the *Animals and Other Decent People's Bank* to deposit his check, word of *las aventuras de*[4] *los cuatro gatos tejanos* spread throughout the little community like a bad case of poison ivy in a hot tub.

Immediately Mayor Hans Hindenharten-Feller proclaimed the next Tuesday as *"El día de*[5] *los cuatro gatos tejanos y Cincinnati el cerdo bailarín."* It wasn't the most grammatically correct name, and wasn't particularly catchy either, but Mayor Hans was a German—*un alemán*—after all. And he hadn't just returned from four days in Mexico, either. Luigi thought it somewhat funny that the mayor began every sentence with the shouted command *"Achtung!"*[6]—as if nobody was ever paying attention to what he was saying.

Which they weren't.

Most of the time, anyway.

Bob the troll told everyone all the mayor really cared about was Cincinnati's new dance studio on Main Street, and Buzzer Louis's big bank account—the one with the one million *pesos* in it.

Luigi responded, "Who cares, Bob¿ We get to ride on top of the big new fire truck in a parade, don't we¿"

The motives of local politicians were of little interest to Luigi. Totally irrelevant compared to a chance to play fireman in front of a big, adoring crowd, anyway.

4. the adventures of
5. The day of
6. Attention!—in German

On this lazy, sunny afternoon while everyone was just waking up from a nap, Bob came back from the mailbox out by the road with a stack of the day's mail.

"Anything besides catalogs in that mail, Bob¿" Buzzer Louis inquired casually.

"Well, let's see here, Buzzy. Here's a Land's End Special Close-Out for Preferred Customers Only and a new big one from L.L. Bean. Hmmm, Frederick's of—oops, that one's mine. Never mind about it. And the Franklin Mint's got one-twenty-fourth scale replicas of the 1954 Nash Rambler—that's kinda cute.

"And, oh, here's a letter from Mexico."

Bob reported the last item so casually it took a minute for its significance to really sink in to the sleepyheads gathered for the daily mail call.

In a delayed reaction like something out of a badly edited black-and-white science fiction film from the 1930s, suddenly everyone came wide-awake and dashed for the table where Bob had dropped the mail.

"Open it, Buzzy! Tell us what it says!" Luisa was truly excited.

"Who's it from, Buzzy¿" Luigi wanted to know.

"Well, let's see here," Buzzer Louis said. "Looks like it's from *la señora Kay Tal* in Mexico City," Buzzer responded. "Let's see what she has to say."

Buzzer began to read the letter, which their new friend had written in the English she had perfected during her adventures with Cincinnati and the four Texan cats.

Dear Cat Friends and Pig,

Sergeant *García* and I thought you might like to hear what has happened since you left us last week.

All the cats from Mérida have been returned to their homes. *El jefe Sonora Sam* finally admitted his daughter—*Margarita (la culebrita)*[6]—was starting to develop evil ways. So he has enrolled her in ethics classes at *La Universidad*[7] *de Camargo.* She will be staying in the city with the brother of *La Cucaracha* and attending classes for six months. We all hope that will straighten her out. *La Cucaracha* says her brother, whose name is *El Escorpión,*[8] will make her behave. Ha, ha.

As a result of the successful mission, *el mayor* has been promoted to *el coronel*[9] (can you guys believe that? Ha!) and *Pablo García* and I have each received nice pay raises.

Well, that's about all the news from here. *¡Ah! Una cosa más.*[10] look at the newspaper clipping I've enclosed.

At least we're rid of him!

Your friend in México
Sra. Kay Tal

"What newspaper clipping, Buzzer?" Luisa was first to speak. And the furrows in her eyebrows gave away an oncoming anxiety attack. "What does it say?"

Buzzer Louis shook the envelope and a folded clipping from

6. the little snake
7. the university
8. The Scorpion
9. The colonel
10. one more thing

La Luz de la Cabeza de México, D.F.[11] dropped out onto the table. Slowly Buzzer unfolded it, glanced at it in horror, and then held it up for everyone to see.

EL GIGANTESCO BÚHO CRIMINAL, FRED-X, ESCAPA DE LA CÁRCEL, SE VA A ROMA[12]

Las fuentes anónimas dicen que él tiene una novia italiana[13]

Below the headline was a large photo of Fred-X, taken just following his arrest by *los federales* in *Progreso*.

"So, that sneaky Fred-X has escaped yet once again," Buzzer sighed. "And he's gone to Rome this time. They speak Italian in Rome, right Dusty¿" Buzz asked the question almost idly, knowing full well the language of Rome was Italian.

"Yes, Buzzer. Italian it is," Dusty replied.

Buzzer just shook his head in dismay.

And as he did, the phone began to ring. Cincinnati strolled over to look at the caller ID and announced the call appeared to be from Europe. From Italy, in fact.

"Does anybody here speak Italian¿" Buzzer asked, not really expecting a response as he headed for the phone.

"Sí, sí signore. Non e problema, amico mio. Parliamo italiano bene, la mia sorella ed io."[14] A voice came from across the room.

"Who said that¿" Bob piped up. "Whatever it was¿"

"L'ho detto bene. Il gattino arancione senza capelli, Luigi

11. The Light from the Head of the Federal District of Mexico

12. Escapes from jail, goes to Rome

13. Anonymous sources say he has an Italian girlfriend

14. Yes, yes sir. Not a problem, my friend. We speak Italian very well, my sister and I.

Panettone Giaccomazza, amici miei," came the answer. *"Tu ricordi bene il nonno Giaccomazza, il marchése di Venezia¿"*[15]

An enthusiastic chorus erupted instantly. "Yea for Luisa and Luigi!!"

Buzzer lifted the telephone receiver, smiled proudly and handed it to Luigi, *il gattino che parla italiano. Molto bene.*[16]

Luigi grabbed the receiver. *"Pronto,"*[17] he said.

---

15. I said it. The hairless, orange kitten, my friends . . . Do you remember well Grandfather Giaccomazza, the Marquis of Venice?

16. the kitten that speaks Italian. Very well

17. Hello

¿ F I N ?
(The End)

O, FORSE UN INIZIO NUOVO?
(Or, Perhaps a New Beginning?)

Gracias, Amigos

Writers of successful books do not create them in an ivory tower somewhere. A good book does not just emerge from a talented writer's word processor without a lot of input, assistance and hard work by many, many other people.

In particular, a bilingual book such as this one requires the scrutiny, ideas, corrections, suggestions and talents of a multitude of persons—not counting the author. Or, in this case, the storyteller and the scribe.

So, Dr. Buford Lewis and I wish to express our sincere thanks and undying gratitude to a bunch of people who helped create, refine and fine-tune—hone, even—this manuscript.

To our faithful reader panel—The first group exposed to both the concept and the initial draft. These long-suffering, hard-reading, mistake-finding, correction-suggesting and downright neat people kept the focus of the manuscript sharp.

In no particular order, we thank our adult readers:

Tom Overton	Houston
Marion Woodfield	Seattle
Julie Fix	Sugar Land, TX

Jim Haynes	Dallas
Richard Brown	Dallas
Barbara Ivancich	Seattle
Margery Arnold, Ph.D.	Los Angeles
Jim Arnold	St. Petersburg
Barbara Arnold	St. Petersburg
D.A. Cooper	Austin
Jonathan Sutter	Kansas City, KS
August Pieres	Houston

And our student readers:

Suzy Groff, Teacher	Bandera, TX
Krista Errington, Teacher	Bandera
George Burns, Teacher	Fredericksburg
Jessica Sutter	Kansas City, KS
Patrick Hicks	Bandera
Dylan Nino	Bandera
Justin Stroesser	Bandera
Tuesday Shaw	Fredericksburg

To the folks at Sunbelt Media—Tom and Virginia Messer, Kris, Amber, Pat, Kim, Jason, Jennifer and the whole gang—thank you. And a very special thanks to our editor, Lynn Adler, for sending us back to the drawing board. Not once. But twice. Good thinking, Lynn.

To our wonderful illustrator, Jason Eckhardt, for giving life and substance to the characters.

And to our Spanish expert, August Pieres, for correcting and polishing our "*dialecto gringo*," turning what we were trying to say into universally understandable *español*. Like all Romance languages, Spanish has many, many dialects. With August's help, we have tried to find the most commonly acceptable translations—words and phrases that would be understood in Mexico, South America, Spain, Cuba, Puerto Rico and the United States—anywhere *donde las gentes hablen algún dialecto del español*.

Any mistakes you may find are mine, alone.

—George Arnold

Glossary and Pronunciation Guide
Common Spanish Words and Phrases

In English	*In Spanish*	Say It Like This
accomplice	*cómplice*	COHM-plee-say
adventures	*aventuras*	ah-ven-TOUR-ahs
again	*otra vez*	OH-trah VAYS
airport	*aeropuerto*	ah-air-oh-PWAIR-toh
airplane	*avión*	Ah-vee-OHN
all	*todo*	TOH-doh
also	*también*	tahm-bee-IHN
always	*siempre*	see-EHM-pray
American	*americano*	ah-mare-ee-CAH-noh
and	*y*	ee
ankles	*tobillos*	toh-BEE-yohs
announcer	*locutora*	loh-coo-TOHR-ah
anonymous	*anónimas*	ah-NOHN-ee-mahs
answer me	*contéstame*	cohn-TESS-tah-may
appearance	*apariencia*	ah-pehr-ee-IHN-see-ah
April	*abril*	ah-BREEL
armadillo	*armadillo*	ahr-mah-DEE-yoh
arms (body part)	*brazos*	BRAH-zohs
at your service (nice to meet you)	*a sus órdenes*	ah soose OHR-deh-nehs
August	*agosto*	ah-GOH-stoh
aunt	*tía*	TEE-ah

In English	In Spanish	Say It Like This
auto racing	*carreras de coches*	cah-RARE-ahs day COH-chehs
bacon	*tocino*	toh-SEE-noh
bad	*malo*	MAH-loh
backpack	*mochila*	moh-CHEE-lah
bag	*bolsa*	BOWL-sah
bank	*banco*	BAHN-coh
baseball	*béisbol*	BAYS-bohl
basketball	*baloncesto*	bah-lohn-SESS-toh
beans	*frijoles*	free-HOH-lehs
bear	*oso*	OH-soh
beautiful	*bella/hermosa*	BELL-ah/air-MOH-sah
beef	*carne de res*	CAR-neh day RAYZ
bell	*campana*	cahm-PAH-nah
belt	*cinturón*	seen-too-ROHN
bicycle	*bicicleta*	bee-see-CLAY-tah
big	*grande*	GRAHN-deh
biggest	*el más grande*	ehl mahs GRAHN-deh
bird	*pájaro*	PAH-hah-roh
black	*negro*	NAY-groh
blouse	*blusa*	BLOO-sah
blue	*azul*	ah-SOOL
boots	*botas*	BOH-tahs
bowl	*tazón/escudilla*	tah-SOHN/ ehs-coo-DEE-yah
bread	*pan*	PAHN
brother	*hermano*	air-MAH-noh
bull	*toro*	TOHR-oh
bullfighter	*toreador*	tohr-ee-ah-DOHR
bus	*autobus*	ah-OO-toh-boose
business	*negocio*	nay-GOH-see-oh
businessman	*hombre de negocio*	OHM-bray day nay-GOH-see-oh
businesswoman	*mujer de negocio*	moo-HAIR day nay-GOH-see-oh
but	*pero*	PAIR-oh

In English	In Spanish	Say It Like This
butter	*mantequilla*	mahn-tay-KEE-yah
cab	*taxi*	TOCK-see
cab driver	*taxísta*	tock-SEES-tah
candy	*bombón*	bohm-BOHN
cap	*garro*	GAHR-roh
captain	*capitán*	cahp-ee-TAHN
car	*auto*	ah-OO-toh
carnival	*carnaval*	cahr-nah-VAHL
castanets	*casteñetas*	cah-sten-YAY-tahs
cat	*gato*	GAH-toh
catnip	*nébeda*	NAY-beh-dah
center	*centro*	SEHN-troh
chair	*silla*	SEE-yah
check	*cheque*	CHEH-kay
cheeks	*cachetes*	cah-CHAY-tehs
cheese	*queso*	KAY-soh
chicken	*pollo*	POH-yoh
chief	*jefe*	HEF-feh
chin	*barbilla*	bahr-BEE-yah
cigar	*cigarro*	see-GAHR-roh
city	*ciudad*	see-yoo-DAHD
climate	*clima*	CLEE-mah
clouds	*nubes*	NOO-behs
coat	*abrigo*	ah-BREE-goh
cockroach	*cucaracha*	coo-cah-RAH-chah
cold	*frío*	FREE-oh
colonel	*coronel*	coh-roh-NEHL
come	*viene*	vee-EHN-eh
come here	*venga aquí*	VEHN-gah ah-KEE
cougar	*puma*	POOH-mah
cow	*vaca*	VAH-cah
crazy	*loco*	LOH-coh
criminal	*criminal*	cree-mee-NAHL
cup	*taza*	TAHT-sah
curve	*curva*	COOR-vah

In English	In Spanish	Say It Like This
dangerous curve	*curva peligroso*	COOR-vah peh-lee-GROH-soh
cycling	*ciclismo*	see-CLEES-moh
dance	*baile*	BY-ee-leh
dancers	*bailarines*	by-lah-REE-nehs
dangerous	*peligroso*	peh-leh-GROH-soh
daughter	*hija*	EE-hah
December	*diciembre*	dee-see-EHM-bray
detective	*detective*	day-teck-TEE-veh
dining room	*comedor*	coh-may-DOHR
dog	*perro*	PAIR-roh
dollar	*peso*	PEH-soh
donkey	*burro*	BOO-roh
door	*puerto*	PWAIR-toh
open the door	*abra la puerta*	AH-brah lah PWAIR-tah
back door	*la puerta trasera*	la PWAIR-tah trah-SAIR-ah
dove	*paloma*	pah-LOH-mah
doubt	*duda*	DOO-dah
no doubt	*sin duda*	seen DOO-dah
dress	*vestido*	vehs-TEE-doh
during	*durante*	doo-RAHN-tay
eagle	*águila*	AH-gwee-lah
eggs	*huevos*	HWAY-vohs
eight	*ocho*	OH-choh
either	*tampoco*	tahm-POH-coh
English	*inglés*	een-GLAYS
escape	*escapa*	ess-CAH-pah
especially	*especiál*	ess-pay-see-AHL
everything	*todo*	TOH-doh
example	*ejemplo*	ay-HEM-ploh
for example	*por ejemplo*	pohr ay-HEM-ploh
excellent	*excelente*	eck-seh-lehn-TAY
excuse	*excuse*	eck-SCOO-say
excuse me	*perdóneme*	pair-DOHN-eh-may,

In English	In Spanish	Say It Like This
	excúseme	eck-SCOO-seh-may
face	*cara*	CAH-rah
fair	*fiesta*	fee-ESS-tah
famous	*famoso*	fah-MOH-soh
father	*padre*	PAH-dray
February	*febrero*	feh-BRAIR-oh
federal police	*federales*	feh-deh-RAH-lehs
final	*final*	fee-NAHL
fingernails	*uñas*	OON-yahs
fingers	*dedos*	DAY-dohs
fireplace	*hogar*	oh-GAHR
first	*primero*	pree-MAIR-oh
fish	*pez*	pehsz
five	*cinco*	SEEN-coh
football	*fútbol norteamericano*	FUET-bahl nohr-tay-ah-mair-ee-CAHN-oh
fork	*tenedor*	teh-neh-DOHR
four	*cuatro*	KWAH-troh
fox	*zorro*	ZOHR-oh
friends	*amigos*	ah-MEE-gohs
frogs	*ranas*	RAH-nahs
fruit	*frutas*	FROO-tahs
funny	*cómico*	COH-mee-coh
get in/enter	*entre usted*	EHN-tray oo-STED
giant	*gigante*	hee-GAHN-tay
gigantic	*gigantesco*	hee-gahn-TESS-coh
girl	*muchacha*	moo-CHAH-chah
girlfriend	*novia*	NOH-vee-ah
glad	*gusto*	GOO-stoh
glad to meet you	*mucho gusto*	MOO-choh GOO-stoh
glass	*vaso*	VAH-szo
glorious	*glorioso*	gloh-ree-OH-soh
gloves	*guantes*	GWAHN-tehs
goat	*cabra*	CAH-brah
goat cheese	*queso de cabras*	KAY-soh day CAH-brahs

In English	In Spanish	Say It Like This
go	*va*	vah
goodbye	*vaya con diós*	VIE-yah cohn dee-OHS
	adiós	ah-dee-OHS
gold	*oro*	OHR-roh
good/well	*bien*	bee-IHN
very good/well	*muy bien*	MOO-ey bee-IHN
good afternoon	*buenas tardes*	BWAY-nahs TAHR-dehs
good day	*buen día*	BWAIN DEE-ah
good night/evening	*buenas noches*	BWAIN-ahs NO-ches
good luck	*buena suerte*	BWAIN-ah SWAIR-tay
good morning/day	*buenos días*	BWAIN-ohs DEE-ahs
granddaughter	*nieta*	nee-AY-tah
grandfather	*abuelo*	ahb-WAY-loh
grandmother	*abuela*	ahb-WAY-lah
grandson	*nieto*	nee-AY-toh
great	*magnifico*	mahg-NEE-fee-coh
green	*verde*	VAIR-deh
gymnastics	*gimnasio*	heem-NAHS-ee-oh
hail	*granizo*	grah-NEE-soh
hair	*pelos*	PAY-lohs
hairless	*sin pelos*	SEEN PAY-lohs
ham	*jamón*	hah-MOHN
hammock	*hámaca*	AH-mah-cah
hands	*manos*	MAH-nohs
hat	*sombrero*	sohm-BRAIR-oh
head	*cabeza*	cah-BAZE-ah
headlights	*lámparas*	LAHM-pah-rahs
heart	*corazón*	cohr-ah-SOHN
helicopter	*helicóptero*	ay-lee-COPE-tehr-oh
hello	*hola*	OH-lah
hello (to answer phone)	*hola/bueno*	OH-lah/BWAIN-oh
help	*ayuda*	eye-YOO-dah
help me	*ayudame*	eye-YOO-dah-may
here	*aquí*	ah-KEE
high	*arriba*	ah-REE-bah

In English	In Spanish	Say It Like This
highway	*camino*	cah-MEE-noh
hills	*colinas*	coh-LEE-nahs
hips	*caderas*	cah-DEHR-ahs
hockey	*hockey*	OH-keh
hog (wild)	*javalina*	hah-vah-LEE-nah
horse	*caballo*	cah-BYE-yoh
hot	*caliente*	cah-lee-IHN-teh
house	*casa*	CAH-sah
How are you?	*¿Como está usted?*	¿COH-moh ess-TAH oo-STED?
How's it going?	*¿Qué tal?*	¿KAY tahl?
I am hungry	*tengo hambre*	TEHN-goh AHM-bray
hungry	*hambriento*	ahm-bree-IHN-toh
I am very hungry	*tengo mucha hambre*	TEHN-goh MOO-chah AHM-bray
I	*yo*	YOH
I understand	*yo entiendo*	YOH ehn-tee-IHN-doh
I don't understand	*yo no entiendo*	YOH noh ehn-tee-IHN-doh
I'm sorry	*lo siento*	loh see-IHN-toh
I would like	*quisiera*	kee-see-AIR-ah
imaginary	*imaginarias*	ee-mah-hee-NAHR-ee-ahs
Indians	*indios*	EEN-dee-ohs
intellectual	*mental*	mehn-TAHL
jacket	*chaqueta*	chah-KAY-tah
jail	*cárcel*	CAHR-sell
January	*enero*	ay-NEHR-oh
job	*trabajo*	trah-BAH-ho
July	*julio*	HOO-lyo
June	*junio*	HOO-nyo
kitchen	*cocina*	coh-SEE-nah
kitten	*gatito*	gah-TEE-toh
knife	*cuchillo*	Coo-CHEE-yoh
last	*final*	fee-NAHL

In English	In Spanish	Say It Like This
leather	*cuero*	KWAIR-oh
let's go	*vámosnos*	VAH-moh-nohs
life	*vida*	VEE-dah
light	*luz*	LOSE
lightning	*relámpago*	ray-LAHM-pah-goh
like	*como*	COH-moh
limousine	*limosina*	lee-moh-SEE-nah
lips	*labios*	LAH-byohs
little	*pequeño*	peh-KAY-nyo
look	*mire*	MEAR-eh
a lot	*mucho*	MOO-choh
luck	*suerte*	SWAIR-teh
good luck	*buena suerte*	BWAIN-ah SWAIR-teh
luggage	*equipaje*	eh-kee-PAH-heh
madam/ma'am	*señora*	sane-YOHR-ah
major	*mayor*	my-YOHR
mama	*mama*	MAH-mah
man	*hombre*	OHM-bray
old man	*viejo/anciano*	vee-AY-hoh/ ahn-see-AHN-oh
many	*muchas*	MOO-chahs
March	*marzo*	MAHR-soh
May	*mayo*	MY-oh
maybe	*tal vez*	TAHL VAYS
medal	*premio*	PRAY-myo
Mexican	*méjicano*	may-hee-CAHN-oh
milk	*leche*	LAY-cheh
minute	*minuto*	mee-NOO-toh
miss	*señorita*	sane-yohr-EE-tah
mission	*misión*	mee-see-OHN
mistake	*corupción*	coh-rup-see-OHN
Monday	*lunes*	LOO-nehs
monkey	*mono*	MOH-noh
moonlight	*luz de la luna*	LOSE day lah LOO-nah
more	*más*	mahs
more or less	*más o menos*	mahs oh MAY-nohs

* Glossary *

In English	In Spanish	Say It Like This
mother	*madre*	MAH-dreh
mountains	*montañas*	mohn-TAHN-yahs
mouth	*boca*	BOH-cah
mister/Mr.	*señor*	sane-YOHR
missus/Mrs.	*señora*	sane-YOHR-ah
my name is	*me llamo*	may YAH-moh
mysterious	*misterioso*	mee-steer-ee-OH-soh
name	*nombre*	NOHM-breh
What is your name?	*¿Cómo se llama?*	¿COH-moh say YOH-mah?
napkin	*servilleta*	sair-vee-YEH-tah
necessary	*necesario*	neh-seh-SAHR-ee-oh
neck	*cuello*	KWAY-yoh
neighbors	*vecinos*	veh-SEE-nohs
nephew	*sobrino*	soh-BREE-noh
new	*nuevo*	noo-AY-voh
niece	*sobrina*	soh-BREE-nah
night	*noche*	noh-CHEH
nine	*nueve*	noo-AY-veh
nothing	*nada*	NAH-dah
November	*noviembre*	noh-vee-EHM-bray
now	*ahora*	ah-OHR-ah
owl	*búho*	BOO-oh
October	*octubre*	ock-TOO-bray
okay	*bueno*	BWAIN-oh
old	*viejo*	vee-AY-hoh
one	*uno*	OO-noh
only	*solo*	SOH-loh
open	*abra*	AH-brah
open the door	*abra la puerta*	AH-brah lah PWAIR-tah
open the window	*abra la ventana*	AH-brah lah ven-TAH-nah
orange (color)	*anaranjado*	ah-nah-rahn-HAH-doh
orange (fruit)	*naranja*	nah-RAHN-hah

In English	In Spanish	Say It Like This
package	*paquete*	pah-KAY-teh
pants	*pantalones*	pahn-tah-LOH-nehs
parents	*padres*	PAH-drehs
parrot	*loro*	LOHR-oh
party	*fiesta*	fee-ESS-tah
path	*senda*	SEHN-dah
pass	*paso*	PAH-SOH
peanuts	*cacahuetes*	cah-cah-HWAY-tehs
perfect	*perfecto*	pair-FECK-toh
pickup	*camioneta*	cah-mee-oh-NET-tah
pig	*cerdo*	SAIR-doh
place	*sitio*	SEE-tyo
plaza	*plaza*	PLAH-sah
please	*por favor*	pore fah-VOHR
police	*policía*	poh-lee-SEE-ah
portable	*portátil*	pohr-TAH-teel
possible	*posible*	poh-SEE-bleh
potato	*patata*	Pah-TAH-tah
pretty	*linda*	LEEN-dah
problem	*problema*	proh-BLAY-mah
queen	*reina*	ray-EE-nah
quickly	*rapidamente*	rah-pee-dah-MEHN-tay
very quickly	*muy pronto*	MOO-ee PROHN-toh
quiet	*silencio*	see-LEHN-see-oh
radio	*radio*	RAH-dee-oh
rain	*lluvia*	YOO-vee-ah
raincoat	*impermeable*	eem-pair-mee-AH-blay
rainy	*lluvioso*	yoo-vee-OH-soh
ranch	*hacienda*	ah-see-EHN-dah
ready¿	*?listo¿*	?LEE-stoh?
red	*rojo*	ROH-hoh
remember	*recuerdo*	ray-KWAIR-doh
report	*informe*	een-FOHR-may
rice	*arroz*	ah-ROHS

In English	In Spanish	Say It Like This
right?	*¿bien? / ¿verdad? / ¿no?*	¿bee-IHN? / ¿vair-DAHD? / NOH?
river	*rio*	REE-oh
road	*camino*	cah-MEE-noh
running	*carrera*	cah-RARE-ah
sacred	*sagrada*	sah-GRAH-dah
sacrifice	*sacrificio*	sah-crah-FEE-see-oh
sad	*triste*	TREE-steh
sailing	*vela*	VAY-lah
saint	*santa(o)*	SAHN-tah(toh)
salad	*ensalada*	ehn-sah-LAH-dah
salt	*sal*	sahl
salted	*con sal*	cohn sahl
satellite	*satélite*	sah-TAY-lee-teh
Saturday	*sábado*	SAH-bah-doh
scarf	*bufanda*	boo-FAHN-dah
scorpion	*escoprión*	ess-core-pee-OHN
sea	*mar*	mahr
seat	*asiento*	ah-see-EHN-toh
second	*segundo*	she-GOON-doh
September	*septiembre*	sep-tee-EHM-bray
sergeant	*sargento*	sahr-HEN-toh
seven	*siete*	see-EHT-tay
shawl	*pañolón*	pahn-yoh-LOHN
sheep	*oveja*	oh-VAY-hah
ship	*barco*	BAHR-coh
shirt	*camisa*	cah-MEE-sah
shoes	*zapatos*	szah-PAH-tohs
shoulders	*hombros*	OHM-brohs
sidewalk	*acera*	ah-SAIR-ah
sir	*señor*	sane-YOHR
sister	*hermana*	air-MAH-nah
sit	*siente*	see-IHN-teh
six	*seis*	sase
sixteen	*dieciseis*	dee-ay-see-SASE
skiing	*esquí*	ess-KEE

In English	In Spanish	Say It Like This
skirt	*falda*	FAHL-dah
skull	*craneo*	CRAH-nee-oh
skunk	*zorillo*	soh-REE-yoh
slowly	*despacio*	des-PAH-syo
more slowly	*más despacio*	mahs des-PAH-syo
snake	*culebra*	coo-LAY-brah
snow	*nieve*	nee-EH-veh
so	*tan*	tahn
soccer	*fútbol*	FUHT-bahl
socks	*calcetines*	cahl-she-TEE-nehs
sofa	*sofa*	soh-FAH
soft	*suave*	SWAH-veh
soldiers	*tropas*	TROH-pahs
some	*cierto*	see-AIR-toh
something	*algo*	AHL-goh
sometimes	*a veces*	ah VAY-sehs
son	*hijo*	EE-hoh
sorry	*siento*	see-EHN-toh
I'm sorry	*lo siento*	loh see-EHN-toh
soup	*sopa*	SOH-pah
sources	*fuentes*	FWEHN-tehs
Spanish	*español*	ess-pahn-YOHL
speak	*habla*	AH-blah
speak more slowly, please	*habla más despacio, por favor*	AH-blah mahs dehs-PAH-syo, pohr fah-VOHR
I don't speak Spanish well	*No hablo español bien*	noh AH-bloh ess-pahn-YOHL bee-IHN
special	*especial*	ess-peh-see-AHL
spoon	*cuchara*	coo-CHAH-rah
stomach	*estomago*	ess-TOH-mah-goh
My stomach hurts	*Me duele el estomago*	may DWAY-leh ehl ess-TOH-mah-goh
stone	*piedra*	pee-AY-drah
storm	*tempestad*	tehm-pehs-TAHD
story	*historia*	ee-STOH-ree-ah
strangers	*extranjeros*	eck-strahn-HAIR-ohs

In English	In Spanish	Say It Like This
stream	*arroyo*	ah-ROY-oh
street	*calle*	CAH-yay
stupid	*estúpido*	ess-TOO-pee-doh
sugar	*azúcar*	ah-SOO-cahr
sun	*sol*	soul
sunlight	*luz del sol*	loos dehl soul
Sunday	*domingo*	doh-MEEN-goh
sure	*bueno*	BWAIN-oh
surprise	*sorpresa*	sohr-PRAY-sah
sweater	*sueter*	SWET-ehr
swimming	*natación*	nah-tah-see-OHN
tablecloth	*mantel*	mahn-TEHL
talk	*habla*	AH-blah
tall	*alto*	AHL-toh
taxi	*taxi*	TOCK-see
taxi driver	*taxísta*	tock-SEE-stah
team	*equípo*	ay-KEE-poh
technician/ repairman	*técnico*	TEK-nee-coh
telephone	*teléfono*	teh-LAY-foh-noh
Texans	*tejanos*	tay-HAH-nohs
temperature	*temperatura*	tem-pair-ah-TOO-rah
ten	*diez*	dee-AYSS
tennis	*tenis*	teh-NEES
terrorist	*terrorista*	tare-ohr-EES-tah
thanks/thank you	*grácias*	GRAH-see-ahs
then	*luego*	loo-AY-goh
there	*allí*	ah-YEE
thin	*delgado*	dello-GAH-doh
this	*esta*	ESS-tah
tiger	*tigre*	TEE-gray
time	*tiempo*	tee-EHM-poh
what time is it?	*¿Qué hora es?*	¿kay OH-rah ESS?
three	*tres*	trace
thunder	*trueno*	troo-AY-noh
Thursday	*jueves*	HWAY-vehs

In English	In Spanish	Say It Like This
today	*hoy*	oi
toes	*dedos de pies*	DAY-dohs day pee-AYS
tomorrow	*mañana*	mah-NYAH-nah
tongue	*lengua*	LEHN-gwah
train	*tren*	trehn
truck	*camión*	cah-MYOHN
trunk (in auto)	*baúl*	bah-OOL
Tuesday	*martes*	MAHR-tehs
turtle	*tortuga*	tohr-TOO-gah
twins	*gemelos*	hay-MAY-lohs
two	*dos*	dose
ugly	*fea*	FAY-ah
umbrella	*paraguas*	pahr-AH-wahs
understand	*entiendo*	ehn-tee-EHN-doh
I understand	*yo entiendo*	yoh ehn-tee-EHN-doh
uncle	*tío*	TEE-oh
university	*universidad*	oo-nee-vair-see-DAHD
until	*hasta*	AH-stah
valuable	*preciosa*	pray-see-OH-sah
vegetables	*verduras*	vair-DOO-rahs
very	*muy*	MOO-ee
village	*aldea*	ahl-DAY-ah
volleyball	*vóleibol*	VOH-lay-ee-bowl
warehouse	*depósito*	day-POSE-ee-toh
water	*agua*	AH-wah
weather	*tiempo*	tee-EHM-poh
wedding	*matrimonio*	mah-tree-MOH-nee-oh
Wednesday	*miércoles*	mee-AIR-coh-lehs
welcome	*bienvenidos*	bee-ehn-vay-NEE-dohs
what?	*¿Qué?*	¿kay?
What's your name?	*¿Cómo se llama?*	¿COH-moh say YAH-mah?
when	*cuando*	KWAHN-doh
where	*dónde*	DOHN-deh

In English	In Spanish	Say It Like This
Where are we going¿	*¿A dónde vamos¿*	¿ah DOHN-day VAH-mohs¿
white	*blanco*	BLAHN-coh
wind	*viento*	vee-EHN-toh
windy	*ventoso*	vin-TOH-soh
with	*con*	cohn
without	*sin*	seen
woman	*mujer*	moo-HAIR
wolf	*lobo*	LOH-boh
world	*mundo*	MOON-doh
wrists	*muñecas*	moon-YECK-ahs
x-ray film	*radiografía*	rah-dee-oh-grah-FEE-ah
xylophone	*xilófono*	see-LOH-foh-noh
yellow	*amarillo*	ah-mah-REE-yoh
yes	*sí*	see
you	*usted*	oo-STED
you're welcome	*de nada*	day NAH-dah
zany	*bufón*	boo-FOHN
zebra	*cebra*	SEB-rah
zero	*cero*	SAIR-oh
zest	*gusto*	HOO-stoh
zip code	*código*	COH-dee-hoh
zoo	*zoológico*	sew-oh-LOGE-ee-coh
zucchini	*calabacín*	cah-lah-bah-SEEN

About the Authors

Storyteller Dr. Buford Lewis, Ph.D.—*The Hillbilly Literati*—(left) checks facts with author George Arnold.

Storyteller—Buford Lewis, Ph.D.

Buford is the only known living canine (a Labrador retriever) that has earned a doctor of philosophy degree. He is professor *emeritus* and holds the *Rin Tin Tin Chair of Letters* at the University of California at Barkley. Prior to taking up residence in the Texas Hill Country, Buford was press secretary to a succession of governors of California.

Author—George Arnold

A late bloomer as an author, George wrote his first book at age 58. *Growing Up Simple: An Irreverent Look at Kids in the 1950s*, with foreword by Liz Carpenter, was an instant success—winning a Silver Spur from the Texas Public Relations Association; the IPPY Humor Award as the funniest book published in 2003 in North America in the Independent Publishers Book Awards; and the Violet Crown Award, presented by the Writers' League of Texas and Barnes & Noble Booksellers as the best work of non-fiction by a Texas author for 2003.

Los Gatos of the CIA: Hunt for Fred-X is his third book.

George and his wife Mary live on a small ranch in the Texas Hill Country. So do Dr. Buford Lewis, Bogart-BOGART, Buzzer Louis, Dusty Louise, Luigi and Luisa Giaccomazza. Together, they raise registered half-Arabian horses, coastal Bermuda hay, and invisible goats.

Yes, they do, too.